MIND GAMES

VONDELL QUEST JACKSON

QUEST PUBLISHING

Cover image by Fernando Serrano via Pexels.

ISBN: 979-8-9920732–0-1

CHAPTER
ONE
CAUGHT

Dark. Cold. It was a typical late-midwestern fall night. Thunder rumbled ominously, rolling across the overcast sky like an encroaching beast. Rain fell in relentless sheets, forming rhythmic patterns that ricocheted off the pavement. Red and blue police lights fused into a pulsating menace, their staccato flare turning the rain into a sporadic, flashing gray. The scene was frenetic—officers and agents moved with urgency; their silhouetted forms blurred by the downpour. The thunder clapped and echoed across the sky, applauding the efforts of the officers and agents in the house surrounded by yellow tape.

The yellow tape fluttered in the gusty wind, a feeble barrier against the morbid curiosity that a crime scene commanded. On one side stood St. Louis police officers, shoulders squared, resolutely segregated from their FBI counterparts. The rivalry between local law enforcement and federal agencies simmered beneath the surface, a relic of past conflicts that had left reputations tarnished and egos bruised. Local officers prided themselves on their intimate knowledge of the community, often viewing the FBI with disdain for their more detached, institutional methods. This created a culture of one-upmanship, a competitive edge that was painfully palpable.

Under a covered section of the driveway, FBI agents congregated, their annoyance evident as they discussed their plans to leave. Their frustrations exacerbated by weather caused them to raise their voices to compete with the ambient noise of the storm. With barely concealed contempt, the agents complain about the local team's inefficacy and murmured about jurisdictional squabbles.

The sudden arrival of a black SUV cut through the tension like a blade, silencing the assembled agents. Detective Alan Richardson exited the vehicle, his features barely discernible under the weak illumination of the flickering streetlight. From the FBI contingent, sneers and whispered jibes rose, led by Agent Jones, a man who epitomized the enmity between the agencies.

"Look who decided to grace us with his presence, if it isn't the Night-walker himself," Jones mocked, loud enough for Richardson to hear. "Left the FBI just to come slumming back here, eh?" He laughed as he continued, "was once one of the FBI finest." Correcting himself, "I mean, Detective Richardson, one of STLPD whiniest, I forgot he couldn't hang with the big boys, so we had to send him packing back to his little kindergarten crew.

Richardson fired back, "How's Subzero? Catch any snowmen yet?" The taunt hung in the air—a nettle meant to provoke. Jones growled, "You're funny. You are a thumbprint away from being in a federal prison. If I find out that you had sabotaged that case, I swear..." Richardson interrupts, "I'm sorry to end this; I would love to stand in a circle with you guys to see who has the biggest case to crack, but I have some work to do. Later!"

Walking away, Richardson's jaw tightened, but he walked with the calm precision that had earned him his moniker, The Nightwalker. "Jones, only you could turn a dead serial killer into a punchline," he retorted, his voice as cold and cutting as the raindrops pelting the ground around them. With an impervious demeanor, he stepped across the invisible demarcation line between local and federal realms. A curious agent leaned over to Agent Jones, "Hey, what's up with Subzero and Det. Richardson?" Agent Jones, in a disgruntled voice, answered back, "Det. Richardson and I were working on a case in Colorado Springs where the FBI was working under-cover in an international drug sting operation. Det. Richardson fell in love with the drug lord's daughter. Although we caught her father, I personally think Det. Richardson helped her escape with all the files and books that magically disappeared—leaving our 5-year case at a standstill until we find where the daughter and the files are.

As Richardson's thoughts spun briefly to the case that had brought him back into this murky world of unresolved atrocities, an officer at the tape broke his reverie. Introductions were made, and Richardson was duly briefed on where to direct his attention inside the house. The officer's words fought to be heard over the incessant rain, each syllable swallowed almost as soon as it was spoken.

The stakes of this particular night could not have been higher. Capturing the Torrential Terror was not just about public safety; it was about a race for glory that both agencies desperately wanted to win. Federal agents hoped this case would stand as a testament to their superior investigative prowess. Meanwhile, the local police, feeling the weight of their intimate knowledge of St. Louis's streets, believed their insight would finally pay off in a public, laudable victory.

The unconditional competition had fostered an environment fraught with tension which was evident from the jarring way both sides monitored each other, every glance a silent accusation of incompetence. Amidst the flickering lights and the storm's wrath, one could forget that this was not a contest but a grave endeavor to catch a merciless killer.

Richardson's attention flicked back to the house, its silhouette a monolith against the storm. The night's relentless clamor underscored the urgency that thrummed beneath the surface, an urgency he could not afford to let falter.

Dismissing the thoughts of rivalry's petty squabbles, he steeled himself for what awaited him inside. The officer held up the tape, and he ducked beneath it, stepping into a world of further uncertainties—one where every shadow might conceal a truth too ghastly to face. The trail of the Torrential Terror beckoned, a macabre puzzle demanding resolution amidst the tempestuous night.

DETECTIVE RICHARDSON PUSHED THROUGH THE FRONT DOOR of the house, shaking off his rain-soaked coat. Lightning illuminated the room momentarily, casting eerie shadows on the walls. Thunder rumbled like a distant beast, a haunting reminder of the storm's ferocity outside. The electric hum of equipment and hushed voices guided Richardson toward the lit area, where activity hinted at the grim discovery within.

Pools of light revealed two bodies: one covered completely, its outline barely discernible beneath the sheet, and another handcuffed and guarded closely by a trio of officers. Richardson's gaze settled on the handcuffed figure, dripping wet and sporting the blank, distant stare of someone in shock. His art had once adorned galleries, shedding light on the human condition, but now Mason Mind appeared as a bewildered part of his tragic canvas.

Detective Matthews, his face etched with tension, stepped forward to greet Richardson. "We've got Mason Mind in custody," he started. "Caught him at the crime scene passed out beside the body."

Richardson's eyes bore into Mason, recognizing the heavy toll the situation was exacting on the young artist. "What evidence do we have against him?" he asked, the question more a reflection of his need for palpable proof than mere curiosity.

Matthews gestured towards a nearby table where evidence bags lay like ghastly trophies. "We found this." He picked up a bag containing a small extraction device and held it up to the dim light. "For removing the eyes. It matches the M.O. of one of our serial killers."

Richardson examined the device without touching it, his mind whirring. The clear surgical precision of the tool contrasted sharply with the delicate, emotive strokes of Mason's artwork. How could someone with a soul deep enough to create such beauty also commit such heinous acts? The storm outside pelted the windows, and Richardson's thoughts rolled with the force of the rain.

"Does it make sense to you?" Richardson's voice cut through the room, laden with skepticism. "A successful artist, dabbling in the grotesque? It doesn't add up for me."

Matthews frowned, determined to support his findings. "We found the sedative device too," he continued, displaying another evidence bag. "And there was an eyewitness, who reported hearing the victim scream before the storm masked all other sounds." He paused, allowing the weight of the facts to sink in.

Richardson took a deep breath, feeling the burden of yet another case weighing down on his already battered psyche. Nights spent in restless pursuit of justice flashed through his mind. Each detail of the current case demanded his scrutiny, but the line between reality and his own demons blurred.

He leaned closer to Matthews, the air thick with tension and rain-tinged humidity. "An eyewitness during a storm? And what about Mason's blackouts during thunderstorms? Could easily be a setup," he argued; needing answers that didn't yet exist. He was craving clarity in a sea of complexities.

Matthews' expression hardened. "We have to follow the evidence, Alan. Regardless of his artistic success or mental state, the facts point to him."

Richardson's resolve stiffened. The glimmer of doubt refused to die in his mind. He traced the outline of the crime scene with his eyes, committing every facet to memory, inching, closer to the truth with each careful observation.

The covered body lay prone, silent amidst the chaos, while Mason's state defied his supposed guilt. Richardson's thoughts flitted back to his FBI days, where misdirection was as rampant as the crimes themselves. The psychological toll gnawed at his resolve and with insomnia as his constant companion, the journey felt more arduous with each passing hour.

Yet, amidst the external storm and internal tempest, clarity was his beacon. Each piece of evidence had to fit the puzzle. His approach was clinical but sympathetic, knowing full well that humanity's worst could lurk behind the most benign facades. The need to untangle Mason's fate from the labyrinth of facts and conjectures spurred his methodical nature.

As Matthews turned to leave, still confident in Mason's guilt, Richardson remained in place, feeling the weight of the moment. He would sift through the noise, decipher the truth trapped beneath layers of assumptions and circumstantial evidence. The storm outside raged on, but within, Richardson began building a foundation of analysis that would outlast the night's fury.

Now alone, Richardson stood amidst the scattered remnants of the evening's horrors, determined to peel back the layers and find the truth. The morass of doubt and conviction intertwined in his mind, threading through the night as surely as the lightning streaked across the St. Louis sky. Lightning illuminated the sky; it changed the night into day. Then as quickly as the lightning came, it was gone. Then again, it became night. It cycled every few minutes, night into day, and then day into night.

LIGHTNING FLASHED THROUGH THE WINDOWS, SLICING THE room into stark contrasts of light and shadow. Detective Alan Richardson stood motionless, his drenched clothes clinging to him as he replayed the sequence of events in his mind. The house was a cacophony of chaos with forensic teams combing through every inch, but he was alone in his thoughts, isolated by a singular focus: the truth.

Water dripped from his hair, mingling with the droplets that seeped from his coat as he peeled it off and tossed it onto a chair. His eyes flitted to Mason Mind, sprawled on a grimy floor, barely conscious. Mason's presence here didn't add up. The snapshots in Richardson's head—the blood, the mutilation, the defiled canvas of human life—formed a collage that screamed for clarity.

His military training, honed to precision, carried him across the room to where the bodies lay. The forensic lights arched over two grotesque displays: one corpse void of an eye and sedated; the other, Mason, barely clinging to life yet somehow implicated. Matthews' earlier explanation echoed in his mind, but Richardson felt an itch between the details, a galling inconsistency he couldn't scratch away.

How could the victim have stabbed Mason after being sedated and mutilated? Richardson's instincts gnawed at him. The tableau before him reeked of something orchestrated. Something did not align with the profiles of either active serial killer. He crouched beside the body, tilting his head to examine the angle of the wounds, the scatter of blood patterns —it was all too precise, too convenient.

A gust of wind battered the windows, the storm outside mirroring the tempest within him. Richardson's experience with the FBI had instilled in him a relentless drive, a near-obsessive need to dissect every fragment of evidence. He thought back to past cases. Those cases where overlooked nuances led to fatal errors. Cases where justice was lost in the mire of haste and assumption. Here, the stakes were high, lives hung in the balance, and the burden of thoroughness bore down on him like an iron weight.

"Eddy, let's move him!" a paramedic's voice pierced through Richardson's reverie. He looked up to see the ambulance crew waiting for his go-ahead. Clearing the fog of his contemplation, he nodded, permitting them to transport Mason to the hospital.

"Make sure officers guard his room door. Notify me the moment he wakes up," Richardson barked, his voice edged with an urgency that brooked no dissent. The ambulance crew nodded, efficiently maneuvering Mason's limp form onto a stretcher.

His gaze lingered on Mason, who stirred slightly, eyelids fluttering, a soft groan escaping his lips. Moments before slipping back into unconsciousness, Mason's eyes opened briefly, confusion and fear etched into his pale features. Richardson watched as the paramedics loaded him into the ambulance, his presence swallowed by the oppressive night.

The crime scene emptied in stages, leaving behind an eerie quiet. Richardson's mind whirred as he surveyed the emptied room. He hated how incomplete the picture felt. Dirty fingernails scraped at the back of his neck in a subconscious gesture, stirring memories of previous failures— cases where misplaced confidence led to misjudgment. The legacy of unsolved atrocities marred his past, each one a blemish on his ethical compass.

He couldn't ignore the possibility that someone else, more insidious, crafted this morbid scene, perhaps even the lurking figure of Hear No Evil, whose grotesque competition with the Torrential Terror had turned his city into a killing ground. With the weight of the city's safety pressing on him, doubting Mason's guilt wasn't a luxury; it was a mandate.

The storm raged outside as if the skies themselves were unleashing their wrath, each thunderclap a somber reminder of their limited time. This wasn't just about solving a crime; it was a race to prevent the next one. Each detail, each minuscule piece of evidence, mocked him, taunting the thoroughness he so desperately wanted to achieve.

Richardson's duty didn't end at arrest; it extended into every shadow, every doubt, and every corner of his investigative principles. The haunting implications of Mason's potential innocence or guilt clawed at his sense of duty. There was an awful vulnerability folded into the endless pursuit of justice. It is a vulnerability that didn't just put his career on the line but his very soul.

He shook himself out of his thoughts. An officer poked his head through the doorway. "Detective, all officers are in place at the hospital. We've secured the perimeter."

Richardson nodded, appreciating the diligence but consumed by the restless pursuit within. "Stay on alert," he said, his voice tinged with an undercurrent of unease. Every decision felt weighted, every moment layered with impending repercussions. Clench-jawed, he made his way back out into the storm, the house's grim interior imprinting on him like an indelible scar as the world outside continued to rage.

Detective Alan Richardson stood near the shattered remnants of a living room, his eyes scanning every detail of the scene for the third time. The ferocious speed and volume of the falling rain were comparable to that of an overstimulated drummer. Each drop hitting the roof like a blunt dagger. His brow furrowed as he replayed everything Detective Matthews had told him. The logic felt forced, as if trying to hammer a mismatched piece into a large, intricate jigsaw puzzle. Could Mason Mind, an artist celebrated for his vivid and humane depictions of life, truly be the Torrential Terror?

Thunder roared through the night, blending with the distant wail of sirens. The yellow crime scene tape fluttered violently in the wind, its stark presence adding a surreal quality to the disorder. Richardson's unease grew; the pit of his stomach filled with bile. Something wasn't right. He knew it from the moment he stepped into the house and felt the malaise hanging in the air, thicker than the smoke from the splintered furniture.

Footsteps pounded the slick pathway behind him. The sound was seasoned and purposeful. Richardson turned just as Chief barreled into the scene, his presence as imposing as the storm outside. Chief's face glistened with rainwater, but his eyes held the fire of impatience.

"Richardson!" Chief's voice cut through the air like a whip. "What's the update?"

Richardson straightened, every inch of his body suddenly rigid. "We've detained Mason Mind. Matthews believes we've got our killer, but..." He hesitated, knowing the weight of his next words.

"But?" Chief's gaze sharpened, and his eyes formed into daggers aimed directly at Richardson. The storm was a reflection of the tempest within the Chief himself, a mixture of frustration and urgency. He had heard about Mason's success and knew the artist's importance both culturally and socially. The media would have a field day—a perfect opportunity to paint the department in whatever shade they preferred, likely a damning one.

"But I have my reservations," Richardson stated firmly. "The evidence feels... too clean. It doesn't match the chaos and brutality we've seen in the Torrential Terror's previous crimes."

Chief stepped closer, the scent of wet leather and stale cigars emanating from him. "Clean or not, we can't afford another headline questioning our competence, especially with the FBI breathing down our necks. You need to get to the hospital and interrogate Mason. Make absolutely sure he's our guy. We can't take any chances."

Richardson could feel the walls closing in, the pressure mounting like the rainfall outside. The Chief's concerns about media exposure were valid, yet Richardson couldn't dismiss the gnawing doubt in his core. His job was to uncover the truth, not to manufacture it for convenience.

"And Richardson," Chief continued, his voice lower but no less intense. "Keep in mind we might be dealing with more than one killer. We don't need another body turning up because we dragged our feet."

A jagged flash of lightning illuminated Chief's stern face, etching lines of deep worry and unyielding resolve. The subsequent boom of thunder seemed to punctuate his command, making the air around them feel all the more oppressive.

Richardson swallowed, each new detail sinking in and festering under his skin. Every weighty command from Chief added another stone to the already precarious pile of his doubts and compulsions. The truth was in the details, in the gaps within Matthew's explanation, in the contradictions that screamed for him to look deeper.

Chief's final warning echoed, a grim reminder of the stakes. Any misstep could not only cost his career but also another innocent life. It was as if he were walking a tightrope in a hurricane, each decision a balance against the relentless winds of doubt and duty.

"Understood, Chief," he replied, his voice steady while his mind churned with an uneasy brew of frustration and determination. In an instant, Chief turned, his departure as brisk as his arrival. He stormed out with his uniformed officers, a whirl of purpose and authority trailing behind him. In one final turn, "And do we have another serial killer out there? I heard the FBI talking about *The Nightwalker*; I can't handle another nutcase right now in my city."

Left alone in the now eerily silent scene, Richardson felt the waves of uncertainty wash over him. He needed clarity, a firmer grasp on the pieces scattered before him. The piercing chill of the night raced through the empty house, amplifying the unresolved questions ricocheting within his mind.

As the rain continued to pound relentlessly, Richardson steeled himself for the next steps. He had to face Mason, peel back the layers of mystery clouding his supposed guilt, and sift through the noise for the truth. His mission was clear: pursue the truth at all costs, even if it meant confronting his own fears and doubts.

CHAPTER
TWO
THE INTERROGATION

D etective Alan Richardson's car tires screeched against the slick pavement as he pulled into the parking lot of City Hospital. The imposing structure loomed in the night, its windows glinting like cold, indifferent eyes. The hospital, usually a place of healing, seemed foreboding against the backdrop of a city plagued by fear. Tension and mistrust dominated in the air, thick as the low, gray clouds that threatened another downpour. Every flicker of the streetlights felt like the city itself flinching away from the horrors that had taken residence within its bones.

Richardson hurried from his car, trench coat flapping against his legs, and pushed through the glass doors of the emergency room. The sharp smell of antiseptic hit him immediately—a sterile mask that couldn't hide the fear etched into the faces of the hospital staff. Murmurs filled the corridors, with a constant refrain of unease. The city had been on edge ever since the serial killings began; the community's trust in law enforcement eroded with each disgusting discovery.

Pulling out his phone, Richardson quickly dialed his office. "Margie, it's Alan. I need a background check on Mason Mind, the artist. Get it to me ASAP," he said, his voice a terse staccato of urgency. He hung up before she could respond, his mind already racing ahead.

Approaching the reception desk, he found an emergency room nurse hurriedly filling out paperwork. "Excuse me," he said, barely reining in his frustration. "I'm looking for information on Mason Mind. He was brought in recently. I need to know his current status and the officers involved in his case."

The nurse glanced up, her eyes wide with stress. "Mason Mind? He was discharged not long ago. Taken to jail by a police officer," she responded, her voice quivering slightly under the weight of her words.

Richardson's jaw clenched. "By which officer?" he asked, his tone sharp, though he softened it just enough to coax a clear answer.

The nurse fumbled with her papers. Smiling, "A tall officer, six feet something, about 220 to 250 pounds, baldheaded, clean-shaved, nice arms, and..." Interrupting, "Sgt. Anderson, that's one of Detective Matthews's boys. Thank you very much, ma'am. By the way, that was a pretty good description. Have you ever taken any criminal justice classes? If not, maybe you ought to think about a career change," he finished laughing. In a shy girl's giggle, "No classes, just thought he was kinda cute."

Richardson's frustration bubbled dangerously beneath the surface, his thoughts flashing back to an unresolved case from his FBI days—a young woman wrongly accused, her life shattered by bureaucracy and miscommunication. He couldn't let this be another one of those times. "Thank you," he said curtly, spinning on his heels and striding towards the exit.

Leaving the hospital, Richardson's mind was a tempest. He drove downtown with a singular focus, each raindrop on the windshield a ticking reminder of his urgency. The rain began to fall in earnest, blurring the outlines of the city and casting the streets in a reflective, wavering light. It was as if the storm itself sought to conceal the secrets hidden in the shadows of buildings and alleyways.

As he navigated through the city, Richardson couldn't shake the nagging doubts about Mason Mind. The artist's blackouts during thunderstorms, the grisly murders, and the vehement insistence on his innocence created a maddeningly complex puzzle. His gut told him there was something off, something that didn't quite fit. Years in the FBI had honed his instincts, making him an insomniac detective perpetually haunted by the cases he couldn't forget.

Pulling up to the precinct, Richardson parked haphazardly and bolted from the car. He took the stairs two at a time, his breath coming in short, controlled bursts. Bursting through the doors, he ignored the curious glances from officers and headed straight for the front desk where Sgt. Henderson sat.

"Where are Matthews and Anderson?" Richardson demanded a mixture of rainwater and sweat dripping from his brow.

Henderson looked up, taken aback by Richardson's intensity. "They're in interrogation with Mason Mind," he replied, his tone cautious.

Richardson's impatience was swelling. He knew he had to tread carefully, the internal dynamics within the precinct as volatile as the storm raging outside. The case was more than another puzzle to be solved; it was a race against time, a fight to save the innocent from becoming collateral damage in a brutal game. Every second wasted was a second lost to prevent further atrocities. With a nod, he pushed past Henderson, his focus still razor-sharp, determined to get to the bottom of this enigma before it was too late.

Richardson's arrival at the precinct was the prelude to a night filled with revelations and confrontations, each step he took resonating with the gravity of the situation. The city, the killers, Mason's plight, and his own past failures interwove into a tapestry of high stakes. Alan braced himself for what was to come, knowing that every action counted and every word mattered. The corridors of the precinct echoed with a mix of faint chatter and underlying tension, setting the stage for the impending clash of wills.

———

MASON MIND WOKE TO THE SOUND OF ANGRY COMMANDS slicing through his groggy haze. The holding cell reeked of sweat and despair, the atmosphere thick and oppressive. When he opened his eyes, the dim light stabbed at them, intensifying the burn. He squinted, trying to make sense of his surroundings. The commands grew sharper and more insistent, echoing off the cold, unforgiving walls.

"Get up!" a voice barked, echoing with authority. Before Mason could gather his thoughts, strong hands gripped his arms. A tall officer yanked him to his feet, nearly causing him to lose his balance. Mason's legs felt weak, half-numb from his supine position on the hard bench. The officer's grip was vice-like, unsympathetic to Mason's disorientation and the sting in his bones.

As they moved down the narrow hallway, the walls seemed to close in, amplifying the officer's heavy footsteps. The passage was shadowy, lined with flickering lights that cast erratic patterns on the floor. Mason stumbled, his vision blurred by the relentless burning in his eyes. Mason noticed that when he rubbed his eyes for clarity, they burned more and that both hands went up when he rubbed his eyes. Harsh voices merged with the distant clamor of machinery, each sound adding to the noise in his head. Realization struck him through the fog—he was handcuffed.

Dazed, Mason tried to focus on the faces surrounding him, but they were fleeting blurs of anger and dismay. The fluorescent lights above highlighted the tension carved into their expressions, lines of stress and resentment deepening around tight lips and narrowed eyes. He caught snippets of shouted words, each phrase another blow to his fragile state.

The officer shoved Mason into a chair with a force that jolted him back to harsh reality. He landed with a thud, the metal of the chair cold against his back. Detective Matthews stood nearby, arms crossed and eyes piercing through the dimness, scrutinizing every twitch of Mason's face. On the periphery, other characters hovered, each a sentinel of judgment.

"Sit down!" Sgt. Anderson thundered, the command reverberating off the walls. Mason flinched, his instinct to comply warring with the instinct to flee. His wrists strained against the cuffs, the metal digging into his skin.

A softer voice broke through the aggressive demands, its tone a velvety contrast. "It's not necessary," the voice said, tinged with a blend of compassion and professionalism. Through the haze, Mason identified the speaker —Simone White, second chair to his lawyer. Her presence was an unexpected balm against the escalating hostility, her words a glimmer of humanity in a sea of accusation.

Detective Matthews, wearing an expression of calculated determination, stepped forward. "Anderson, leave," he said, authority emanating from his every syllable.

Anderson's face twisted with reluctance, a silent battle of wills unfolding between the two men. Finally, with a tense nod, Anderson turned on his heel and exited the room; his departure left a void filled with the charged silence of the remaining figures. Detective Matthews stepped out quickly to console his young prodigy.

As Mason's eyes adjusted to the shifting lights, confusion mingled with fear. He strained to recognize the faces and to make sense of the collage of expressions that surrounded him. The sting in his eyes intensified, beyond the physical pain to a soul-deep ache. And then he saw it in a two-way mirror on the wall behind everyone—red streaks against his skin, staining his clothes. Horror wrapped around his mind like iron chains.

"What is this?" he demanded, his voice cracking under the weight of his need for answers. His bewildered gaze darted from face to face, seeking an explanation in the cold, impassive eyes of his captors.

The mixture of his helplessness and their interrogation techniques was a potent brew, simmering with the potential to boil over at any moment. Here, the very air seemed to conspire against him, thickening with an almost tangible intensity. Every breath he took was a struggle, every exhalation a surrender.

In this crucible of power dynamics, Mason's disorientation was complete, his thoughts a fragmented mosaic. He was acutely aware of his vulnerability, the sharp contrast between his position and the intimidating presence of his accusers. Amidst his internal turmoil, he couldn't shake the feeling that the red on his skin symbolized something more than just a mishap—it was a mark of his entanglement in a scenario he scarcely understood.

As the final shards of recognition began to piece together, the world around Mason became a whirlpool of raw emotion and unyielding suspicion. He was an isolated figure in a hostile landscape, desperate for clarity in a situation defined by imminent danger and shrouded motives.

<hr />

MASON BLINKED THROUGH THE HAZE THAT CLOUDED HIS thoughts, trying to make sense of the blurry figures around him. His head throbbed, the relentless ache a constant reminder of the previous night's chaos. The interrogation room felt more like a frozen tomb than a place of questioning; the stark white walls only intensified his disorientation. He struggled to focus on the man seated across from him—Walter Wright III, whose name surfaced amid the fog in Mason's brain, introduced with a calm authority reminiscent of a season-long veteran.

"Mr. Mind, I'm Walter Wright III, and this," Walter motioned to the woman beside him, "is Simone White, my assistant. Your uncle, Eric, hired us to represent you. We're here to help."

Mason's heart skipped a beat; the mention of his uncle brought back a rush of memories dripping in warmth and comfort from simpler times. Eric had been his rock, always believing in his talent and his innocence. But now, those memories clashed violently with the present, with the suffocating reality of handcuffs biting into his wrists and the accusing glares of strangers.

As Walter spoke, explaining the seriousness of the accusations and the support system aligning behind him, Mason couldn't help but wrestle with an overwhelming mixture of hope and dread. Each word from Walter drummed into his consciousness, attempting to pierce through the chaotic mess in his head. He was advised to cooperate, to speak only with Simone regarding his thoughts, and everything else seemed secondary—a blur against the backdrop of his raging, tortured mind.

Just as Mason began to steady himself, the door swung open with an ominous creak. Detective Richardson entered with the calm precision of someone who had cracked countless cases, a placid look masking steely determination. His presence was almost suffocating, the aura of authority making Mason's breaths feel shallow. The room grew colder.

"We need to get through this," Richardson began methodically, "Mason Mind, you are being charged with multiple counts of murder." Richardson's voice indicated neither doubt nor sympathy, only the rigid truth of the law.

Suddenly, a thousand voices screamed within Mason's head, the gravity of the words slamming into him. His pulse quickened—it was a cacophony, a whirlwind of fragmented images, and roaring accusations. Richardson continued, reading his Miranda rights with a cadence as rhythmic as a judge's gavel, each word a verdict in Mason's unsettled mind. Panic rose like bitter bile in his throat; every muscle in his body tensed against the onslaught of emotions threatening to pull him under.

"Stop! Please, just stop!" Mason's voice cracked, his desperation spilling into the cold air. But it seemed to fall on deaf ears.

Detective Matthews, with a face etched by years of hardened service and eyes that blazed with zealous intensity, barged into the room, slamming a folder onto the table. Photographs spilled out like dark secrets unleashed, marring the sterile environment with raw, unfiltered horror. Matthews' accusatory tone roared through the air, painting Mason as more than merely guilty—as the embodiment of monstrosity.

"Look at these!" Matthews spat, thrusting photos in front of Mason. Each image displayed abominable scenes—portraits of horror Mason could hardly fathom. Blood, mutilation, despair. The victims stared back, their lost lives haunting the shadows of his mind. Each photograph was a moral assault, a question he didn't know how to answer.

"That's enough!" Simone White's voice cut through the tension with a calm yet firm insistence. She approached Mason with measured steps, her professionalism a balm to the chaos. "We'll continue this discussion on Monday morning," she declared, her tone brokering no argument.

But Mason's confusion only deepened. The room felt like it was closing in on him, the walls pressing with the weight of his unspoken fears and questions. "What am I supposed to do until then?" he asked, his voice trembling with a mix of fury and helplessness.

Simone met his eyes, her gaze filled with a compassionate yet pragmatic resolve. "You'll be held here in confinement, Mason. There's nothing more to do tonight."

Detective Matthews, still radiating anger, confirmed with a nod. "Indeed. You'll stay put until we figure this out."

The room fell into a heavy silence, broken only by the erratic rhythm of Mason's breaths. He searched their faces, hoping for any sign of certainty, but found only the reflection of his own tumultuous thoughts. Every gaze felt like a judgment, and as he tried to reconcile his innocence amidst the labyrinth of accusations, the enormity of the night's revelations engulfed him.

With finality, the scene drew to a close. The gavel of implied accusations lingered, each tick of the clock underscoring the vast chasm between Mason's internal chaos and the external verdict rushing to meet him.

SGT. ANDERSON'S GRIP ON MASON'S ARM WAS IRONCLAD, delivering him towards the holding cell. Their path, illuminated by flickering fluorescent lights, cast eerie shadows on the walls. Mason stumbled, struggling to keep pace. The hallway seemed endless, a tunnel leading to nothingness.

"You really think you can play innocent, don't you?" Anderson's voice, dripping with disdain, sliced through the silence. His face, set in a grim mask, radiated determination forged by years of dealing with crooks who'd tried to wiggle out of consequences.

Mason's mind spun, grappling with a reality that felt like a distorted dream. He couldn't even remember how he got here. "I don't know what you think I've done," he said, his voice shaking but sincere. "But I'm not who you think I am."

Anderson's grip tightened, his gaze piercing through Mason. "Save it. We found you at the scene. Your alibis are flimsy, just like your story. You fit the profile—the blackouts, the erratic behavior."

As they continued down the hallway, the discord of the precinct buzzed around them. Harsh fluorescent lights hummed and reflected on the cold tiles, matching the chill seeping into Mason's bones. He felt the weight of public opinion, a society fearful and eager to see justice served, ready to brand him a monster.

"There's always evidence, Mason," Anderson pressed, his tone akin to a schoolteacher reprimanding a wayward student. "The numbers don't lie. Your friend Stephen Carter, the letter in your studio, the timing of the storms. It's all there."

Mason's heart pounded in his chest. Disjointed memories fluttered like moths trapped in a jar, fragments of faces and places that made no coherent sense. "That doesn't mean it's me," he pleaded, desperation choking his words. "Mistakes happen. Innocent people get framed."

"Innocent?" Anderson barked a bitter laugh. "You know how many families are out there, waiting for closure? The pressures on us to solve this, and no one's forgetting who they've lost." The sergeant's eyes flickered with a mixture of obligation and weary anger as he navigated the pressure cooker environment, where every unsolved case was a blow to the force's credibility.

As they reached the door to Mason's holding cell, Anderson stopped, staring hard at the artist. "You think it's all some misunderstandings? Fine. Here's something to mull over. Every murder, every storm—it all ties to you like clockwork. You've got a pattern, Mason. A sick, twisted pattern."

Mason's head swam. He swallowed hard, trying to steady himself. "If... if their theory was wrong," he began, his voice a fragile whisper, "what would it take to prove it? A puzzle with no clear pieces, something you couldn't fit."

Anderson's eyes narrowed, his patience wearing thin. "What kind of hypothetical nonsense is that?"

Mason sighed, feeling the cuffs dig into his wrists. "If you had three pieces of a puzzle—one suspect, one crime scene, and one improbable coincidence—how would you solve it?"

The sergeant paused, his fist clenching with barely contained rage. "You think this is some kind of game?" he spat. "This isn't one of your art projects. People are dead. Their families are suffering."

He thrust Mason into the cell, the cold metal of the bars biting into Mason's back. "Just shut up and think about what you've done," Anderson snapped, stepping back. Mason felt a chill from his toes to the top of his head. He saw the end of his life flash right before him, and it ended with his face wrapped around Sgt. Anderson's fist. He quickly entered the cell and instantly felt his end. Maybe the cell wasn't a bad place to be currently. What was before a possible misunderstanding to him was now his reality.

But behind Anderson's frustration was a hint of uncertainty, a seed of doubt gnawing at him. He hated loose ends, and Mason seemed less like a malevolent figure and more like a man lost in his own mind.

Alone in the cell, Mason slumped to the floor. He could hear the echoes of society's condemnation, their voices a chorus of fear and judgment. He closed his eyes, the tears of frustration and fear leaking out. The fluorescent lights buzzed on, indifferent to the turmoil beneath them.

CHAPTER
THREE
BACKGROUND

Early Monday morning, the precinct was quiet, a calm before the chaotic storm of the day. Margie sat alone in the fluorescent-lit room, her eyes weary but determined. The stale scent of old coffee lingered, mixing with the distinct aroma of ink from the fax machine in front of her. As the machine spat out page after page, she could feel the pulse of the precinct, a place where lives had intertwined with crime in ways she knew too well.

Margie had been an investigator for over a decade, molded by the turbulent tides of countless cases. Each discovery and lead had left an indelible mark on her soul, etching lessons in grit and resilience. One case, in particular, had always haunted her—the mistranslation of evidence leading to a wrongful accusation, shattering a family and her own sense of moral clarity. It was this memory that honed her vigilance, fueling her meticulous nature. She knew the stakes; she knew the weight of every decision.

The pages continued to stream out, and Margie's hands trembled. Suddenly, amidst the routine documents in an article dated February 24, 2007, a phrase jumped out: "Mason Mind, suspect in UCLA campus killing, acquitted due to lack of evidence." Her heart skipped a beat, a cold dread creeping up her spine. The remnants of her past haunted her,

knowing well how easily truth could slip through the cracks, leaving innocent lives desolated.

"Not again," she whispered to herself. The tremor in her hands grew
as she yanked the wire free from the machine. She felt the icy fingers of the
past gripping her heart, memories of that harrowing wrongful accusation
swirling in her thoughts. She couldn't afford another mistake, not one that
echoed so ominously through the corridors of her past experiences.

She suppressed a shiver, a steely resolve taking hold. She darted
towards her desk and picked up the phone. As her fingers danced over the
numbers, her mind raced back to Alan Richardson. Over the years, they
had carved out a unique camaraderie amidst the precinct's chaos. Richardson's instincts had been their beacon of light in more cases than she cared
to count. She remembered the times his intuition had guided them to
breakthroughs, stories shared over countless late-night coffee cups, their
bond solidified in the relentless pursuit of justice.

Margie's trust in Richardson was unshakeable, born of countless
collaborations. She had seen what magic his mind could weave and how his
pattern recognition could untangle the densest webs of deceit. She knew
deep down, if anyone could make sense of this discovery, it would be Alan.

With urgency, she punched in Richardson's number, each beep
echoing her mounting anxiety. As she waited for the call to connect, her
thoughts spiraled. Richardson hated early morning calls; she knew he had
likely worked through the night, as was his habit. Yet the gravity of her
discovery surpassed any concern for disrupting his rest. She had to break
through the fog of exhaustion that likely enveloped him.

The phone's shrill ring cut through the quiet of Richardson's dim
office miles away, pulling him from the grasp of an uneasy sleep. In his
mind's eye, Margie's anxiety played out vividly. What if this was the key to
everything? What if delving into Mason Mind's past provided the answers
they sought for the current wave of murders? The thought gnawed at her,
heightening her heartbeat into a frantic drumroll.

Margie's mind raced through the details again, Mason Mind's name
glaring at her from the page. Born in 1987, the youngest of six kids, he was
a prodigy-turned-pariah, fated to dance between the brilliance of his talent
and the shadows of suspicion. How many others had fallen through the
cracks as he might have, caught between their genius and society's harsh

judgment? The tragic irony of an artist whose mind was both a gift and a curse weighed heavily on her.

Throughout her career, Margie had seen how mental health issues could twist perceptions, be they of the individual or society at large. Mason's severe anxiety disorder and stress-induced blackouts painted a picture of a tormented soul. The facility stints, the weekly therapy sessions —they were the efforts of a man trying to stitch his fractured reality back together. Yet the world around him, unforgiving and ever-watchful, had its own tale to tell. Margie understood that delicate balance all too well— the fine line between genius and madness.

Her fingers gripped the phone tighter as the call began to connect. Richardson's familiar, gravelly voice broke through the static, still tangled in remnants of sleep. She could almost see him rubbing his eyes, shaking off the exhaustion that defined his relentless pursuit of justice.

Margie swallowed hard, her mouth dry. She knew she had to convey the significance of this discovery, to pull Alan out of his grogginess and into the disturbing clarity she now faced. Their past collaborations flashed before her eyes, moments where Richardson's keen insights had redirected their paths. She needed him now, more than ever, to unravel the tapestry of Mason Mind's life and its ominous intersections with their present.

The urgency thrummed through her, pushing her over the edge into that familiar, intoxicating realm of the hunt. This was more than a lead; it was a lifeline, and she had to trust that Alan would grasp it with the conviction she'd come to rely on.

EARLY MORNING LIGHT FILTERED THROUGH THE HALF-CLOSED blinds, casting soft, horizontal shadows across Alan Richardson's cluttered desk. The scent of stale coffee lingered faintly in the air, mixing with the subtle, persistent hum of the police scanner. Alan lay sprawled on his old leather couch, exhaustion from the previous night's relentless work evident in his closed eyes and slightly parted lips. His shabby office felt like a cave—sanctuary and tomb alike.

The shrill ring of his phone shattered the fragile silence, a jarring sound that jolted Alan awake. He groaned, fumbling for the device. "Hello?" he muttered, his voice gravelly with sleep.

"Alan, it's Margie," crackled the urgent voice on the other end, static underscoring the tension.

Alan blinked against the persistent pull of sleep, forcing himself upright. His thoughts were still sluggish, tangled in the web of fatigue woven by countless nights of restless pursuit. "Margie, what's so important?" His words dripped with irritation but were softened by the genuine trust he placed in her. They had worked together for years, a friendship and professional bond that had withstood the flames of high-stakes cases and the chilling solitude of late-night stakeouts.

"Listen to me, Alan." Margie's tone brooked no argument, urgency giving it an edge sharp enough to cut through his drowsiness. "It's Mason Mind. Born in Long Beach, the youngest of six kids, an artist who got a scholarship to UCLA."

Alan rubbed his eyes, shaking off sleep. Memories of cases past flickered in his mind, drawing connections between genius and madness, brilliance and torment. He could almost see the sun-drenched streets of Long Beach and feel the pressure of burgeoning talent weighed down by expectation and the constant struggle for recognition amidst a large family. "Is this about that campus murder?" The question was more statement than inquiry. Richardson's mind always sought the patterns—the neat, albeit abhorrent, dovetailing of one case's tail into another's head.

"Yes," Margie confirmed, voice trembling slightly. "A girl had been killed—eyes removed, sedative puncture on her hand. Mason was a suspect but got off due to lack of evidence. His alibi was airtight."

Alan straightened, the fog of exhaustion finally beginning to lift. The heinous details—repulsive as they were—added clarity, drawing stark lines between those past events and the current wave of violence sweeping through the city. The severity of the crime mirrored the monstrous echoes of the ongoing cases they were buried in.

"And then?" he prompted, the word filled with an anticipatory dread that swallowed everything in its path.

"He had a nervous breakdown. Severe anxiety disorder, stress-induced blackouts, committed briefly to a psych facility," Margie's voice softened, as though treading lightly on the thin ice of Richardson's patience. Her veneer of usually composed demeanor cracked under the weight of her findings. Perhaps it was a reflection of Richardson's own unspoken fears—

a fear that the world was an artistic canvas smeared with blood and suffering, a harsh critique of human frailty.

Richardson's heartbeat quickened, his mind leaping through corridors of memory and instinct. Artists and mental health—the equation was fraught with peril. How many times had he stared into the abyss of someone's tormented soul, genius spiraling into madness? It was an unwelcome but familiar specter at the edge of his investigations.

"He owns a gallery now, Quest Art Gallery downtown. And Alan, listen carefully—it connects to the recent murders," Margie said, her voice painting strokes of dread across the silence. "The precision of the cuts, the use of sedatives... it's too similar to ignore."

He felt the air grow colder, the pressing weight of unspoken truths. His past cases had taught him that the meticulous recycling of such brutal methods was no coincidence; it was a signature, a dark artistry replicated with chilling accuracy. Yet nothing concrete tied Mason to the current killings.

Alan cradled the phone tighter, a tactile reassurance as though it could comfort against the mounting storm within him. Each piece of the puzzle Margie provided felt like another agonizing step towards a grim truth he wasn't sure he wanted to reach.

"Tell me everything," Alan commanded, his tone shifting from weary indifference to razor-sharp focus. In moments like these, his nickname "Nightwalker" was earned—not in the shared light of day but in the solitary darkness where devils danced.

Margie didn't need further prompting. She recounted Mason's life with clinical precision—the whispers of erratic behavior, the sudden silence of his spotless record post-college, and the unsettlingly timed spikes in suspicious activity around his gallery years later. Each detail was a thread in a tapestry stained by both brilliance and horror.

Alan couldn't shake the rising desperation clawing at Mason's edges, the suffocating burden of mental illness painted over by societal stigma and unresolved trauma. How did it feel, he wondered, to be trapped in lapses of time, only to resurface into an unrelenting reality where the only evidence of your existence was the carnage left behind?

His thoughts turned to Margie, the steady anchor of his investigative storms. Their partnership had been forged in the fires of complexity and human fallibility, and it was this shared history that allowed them to operate with an almost telepathic synchronization.

"Got it," Alan said finally, his fingers tightening around the phone. He felt the weight of their mission, the pressing need to dissect the bloody history that tied them to Mason Mind. The office, once a tomb, seemed now a crucible, refining his purpose into a single, unyielding drive for justice.

ALAN TOOK A DEEP BREATH, HIS EYES ROAMING AROUND THE cluttered office. Crime scene photographs pinned to the walls captured his attention, each a fragment of a horrifying mosaic. His desk teemed with case files, their edges curling from age and handling. The cold, clinical sheen of the laminated photographs contrasted sharply with the raw emotion they portrayed—faces locked forever in expressions of fear and pain.

Margie's voice buzzed in his ears over the phone, propelled now by fervor he hadn't heard from her before. "You know, Alan, Mason's gallery was opened just months after he was released from the psych facility. He's been under the radar, but there've been whispers—murders, similar to the one at UCLA seventeen years ago. The victims... Alan, all young females, eyes mutilated, sedative marks found."

Richardson's mind skated over the cryptic connections, the web of violence spinning ever tighter. The hint of sedatives made his skin crawl, chillingly similar to signs he'd seen in past cases. He felt a nagging sensation that Mason's artistic pursuits were cloaking something more sinister. The unsettling detail that a creative genius grappled with blackouts and anxiety hinted at a fractured psyche, an internal landscape teeming with dissonance and fear.

"Go on, Margie," he urged, feeling his pulse quicken.

"Mason's behavior was erratic; students and teachers barely whispered it, but the pattern—Alan, the pattern remains. No one has looked deeper until now," she continued, her voice a blend of excitement and dread.

Richardson's thoughts traveled backward to other investigations—cases where he had dug into the psyches of killers. He remembered the harrowing intersections of creativity and cruelty: artists whose inner demons bled into their canvases. One case in particular resurfaced of a sculptor whose masterpieces were darkly inspired by scenes of torture witnessed in his youth. Alan recalled feeling both awe and revulsion, the line between genius and madness blurring disturbingly.

Margie continued, her fervor feeding his growing realization. "The victims —several of them—had no apparent connection. But Alan, all of them, at some point, had stepped into Mason's gallery. It was a place that drew them in, perhaps drawn as moths to a flame, unaware of the smoldering danger."

A chill settled in Richardson's bones. His fingers tapped anxiously on the edge of his desk. The photographs seemed to pulse with a hidden rhythm, each crime a silent scream waiting to be understood. He thought of the gallery tucked into the folds of downtown, an oasis of beauty masking the stench of possible decay. Mason's psychological ruin and his past traumas echoed hauntingly in Richardson's mind, vibrating with the possibility of unresolved rage and obsessive cycles.

As Margie detailed the profiles of the victims, Richardson leaned back, feeling the silhouette of recognition carving into his consciousness. All young, all captivated by art, their lives stolen and expression eradicated. The sealed case, the minor's status—these were pieces shrouded in secrecy, providing an almost tangible weight to his unfolding revelation.

Richardson's past experiences offered a painful backdrop—faces of the lost, trial verdicts, courtroom testimonies—all swimming up to haunt him. He remembered a particular boy, a promising young violinist whose mental breakdown led to a brutal crime spree. Richardson's attempts to unravel the threads of the boy's life yielded a tapestry of hidden abuse, untreated mental illness, and societal neglect. Everything he'd learned from those encounters now sharpened his focus on Mason, illuminating the tragic, damning intersections of mental health and genius.

"Mason's record had a gap, but not his intentions," Margie concluded, almost trembling through the line.

The realization struck Alan with overwhelming clarity. The gallery was more than a place of beauty; it was a stage set for horrors cloaked in grace and form. Mason's history was a symphony of chaos, mental breakdowns harmonizing with brutal precision, creating a chilling composition only the most damaged of minds could orchestrate.

"We need to act fast, Margie. His history—his patterns—this can't be a coincidence." Richardson's voice was a tight whisper suffused with urgency.

Margie, silent for a moment, let the gravity of his words settle. "You're right. It all fits, doesn't it? The gallery... It's more than just a front for his art. It's a beacon for his darkness."

Alan cradled the phone tighter, the tendrils of anxiety coiling within him, memories of faces he couldn't save flashing before his eyes. The evidence wasn't just on paper; it was in the emotions, the patterns, and the dark spaces that connected them like constellations of despair. How many more victims lay unseen, their stories untold, eclipsed by the deceptive allure of artwork?

Leaning back in his chair, he absorbed the full weight of the revelations, the sense of duty pressing heavily upon his chest. The sealed case, the whispers, the obsessive patterns—all pointed to an inescapable truth that demanded action. Mason Mind was not just an artist ravaged by his past; he was a predator, concealed under the veneer of culture and creativity. Richardson's resolve solidified, root deep, ready to dismantle the gruesome tapestry strand by bloody strand.

With every passing moment, Richardson's compulsion for justice burned brighter, the intricate connections forming a path he knew he had to follow before another life flickered out, unseen.

ALAN STOOD UP, HIS LIMBS HEAVY YET POWERED BY A SUDDEN surge of purpose. His mind looped back to Margie's urgent tone as he thanked her, the weight of gratitude and urgency in his voice. Driven by a sense of looming justice, he snatched his coat off the back of his chair, the fabric whispering against his skin as he moved quickly, driven by a sense of looming justice. Each step was a beat as he headed for the door, the years of being on the force drumming familiarity yet disparity into every motion.

Alan slammed the door behind him, his pulse quickening, matching the rapid tap of his boots on the weathered stairs. He bolted towards his black-on-black Chrysler 300S, a loyal beast that had seen countless rides through the serpentine streets of the city. Sliding into the driver's seat, he felt the leather conform to his frame—a brief comfort amidst the storm brewing in his mind.

The ignition roared to life under his grip, and he sped out onto the streets, the city awakening under the first light of dawn. Buildings and storefronts flickered by shadows leaping from every corner as if hiding the truths he sought. His heart drummed in sync with the engine's rumble, a symphony echoing his internal resolve. The cases he didn't solve, the victims he couldn't save—they floated like ghosts before his eyes as he steered the car with sharp determination.

Richardson's mind whirled back to his early days, when enthusiasm and rookie mistakes collided in the gritty alleyways of justice. He remembered a particular case—a girl, no older than fifteen, who had been found too late because he had been too slow. A chill settled over him, a scar from the past surfacing to remind him why he couldn't afford to falter now. Mason Mind's case bore the haunting echoes of that past failure, and he couldn't bear to let history repeat itself.

The streets blurred into streaks of gray and muted colors, a monotony broken by random flashes of life. Richardson's gaze flicked to the review mirror, the world behind and ahead of him merging in a fluid dance. He recalled his mentors' words—those who had taught him the delicate balance between instinct and procedure, those voices that now served as a steadying force as he navigated crises such as these. He was a detective shaped by each ghostly whisper of unsolved cases and every etched line in the files that cluttered his desk.

He muttered to himself, the words a mantra of resolution. "Not this time. Not today." His grip tightened on the steering wheel, knuckles blanching with the force of his conviction. Alan wasn't only fighting the crimes but the specters of his own imperfections, the endless loop of the what-ifs that gnawed at his sanity in quieter moments.

The drive was a narrow tunnel filled with fleeting visions of past mistakes and hard-earned triumphs. Mason Mind's fractured life painted itself in vivid hues before Richardson's eyes—an artist once poised for greatness, now shadowed by accusations and mental turmoil. Could the fragments of Mason's shattered world somehow link to the present horrors they faced? Richardson's gut twisted with the need to understand, to peel back layers until only the raw truth remained.

The city's pulse quickened as he neared the courthouse. His mobile handheld radio crackled, a static-laced voice announcing the presence of a mob demanding justice. Richardson's jaw set tight, the courthouse emerging like a fortress on the horizon, its steps crowded with a sea of anger and frustration.

As adrenaline flooded his veins, Richardson's thoughts narrowed into a singular focus. The world around him shrank—ambient noises fell silent, and all that remained were his racing thoughts and the steady beat of his heart. He pictured the chaos at the courthouse, the faces contorted in cries for justice, each sign a testament to societal unrest. Pulling closer, he felt the subtle weight of his mission multiply, intensifying with every footfall on the courthouse steps.

In front of him, the massive granite building stood, standing as a silent judge itself. Richardson's burdens were more than personal; they were tangential to the lives of those demanding change, those who had lost faith in a system he still believed could serve justice. For Alan, this case was more than lines on paper or patterns in behavior—it was a chance to protect and to serve, to bridge the gap between chaos and order.

Just as he approached the final barricade, the clamor of the crowd hit him in a wave. He knew he was stepping not only into the court-house but into the eye of a storm—a convergence of past failures, present demands, and future hopes. Richardson's resolve solidified; each step was a promise to himself and to the victims of both the past and present. Today, he would not let shadows win. Justice was not merely a duty; it was the heartbeat of every step he took toward that courthouse door.

The city's hum rose to a crescendo as Richardson parked and stepped out, feeling the gravity of the moment tighten around him like a vice. He would peel back the layers until truth stood naked and unmarred. With unyielding determination, Richardson readied himself to confront what-ever awaited him beyond those stone steps, every fiber of his being attuned to the pursuit of justice.

RICHARDSON PARKED HIS BLACK-ON-BLACK CHRYSLER 300S IN the nearest available spot and stepped out into the crisp morning air. The courthouse loomed before him, its imposing stone façade stark against the dusky sky. Below its grand steps, a sea of protesters churned, their signs bobbing like agitated waves.

"Justice for All!" "Mental Health Matters!" "No Artist Above the Law!" The slogans swallowed Richardson as he navigated through the throng. He could see the intensity in the eyes of the protesters, their collective anger like a smoldering fire ready to ignite. The case of Mason Mind had split the city, sewing a rift between those who saw him as a misunderstood genius and those who condemned him as a manipulative monster.

Richardson waved to a cluster of uniformed officers standing off to the side, their gazes sweeping the crowd like hawks. "We need barricades up now!" His voice cut through the clamor. "Keep them across the street, and make sure no one's getting hurt!"

One officer nodded, pulling out a radio to dispatch the necessary reinforcements. The memory of other high-profile cases surged up through Alan, their shadows casting long, unsettling silhouettes over his current mission. He recalled the public uproar following the arrest of a renowned photographer years ago—accused of a similar crime but never convicted. The protests then had been vicious, heartfelt, and utterly chaotic. The event had ended in riots, and Alan knew he had to prevent such an outcome today.

As the officers distributed metal barricades along the perimeter, Richardson's attention drifted back to the courthouse doors. Hardened lines set in his face, reflecting the weight of an inner conflict. Mason Mind was more than just another suspect. He was a man whose art had captured the very soul of the city—a city now angrily divided.

A smattering of peace signs dotted the crowd, echoes of a time when protests were synonymous with harmonious change, not the angry shouts they had devolved into. Richardson's mind flashed through past headlines: "Artistic Prodigy or Sinister Manipulator?" "Court Case Shocks the Nation, Mental Health at Forefront," "UCLA Reopens Old Wounds." Each article grabbed the public's attention, polarizing opinions and making the case more about public perception than the hard facts.

Richardson's hand went to his hip, gripping the reassuring bulk of his notepad. The notes within it mapped out a series of violent puzzles waiting to be pieced together. Turning to the nearest officer, he barked, "I want a clear path to the courthouse. Let the media and essential personnel through, but keep the demonstrators back."

As the officer relayed his instructions, Alan couldn't shake a persistent thought. He remembered the disbelief that had marked the acquittal of another artist years ago and how the media had swarmed the courthouse steps just like today. The trial had left indelible scars on the community and had cast suspicion like a net over those struggling with mental health issues. Alan understood the stakes: Mason's case threatened to reopen these old wounds, making the need for justice and clarity more crucial than ever.

The crowd's tempo escalated, chants rising in unison, a crescendo of collective voices demanding justice. The officers moved methodically, ushering the protesters back while erecting the necessary barricades. Richardson's focus sharpened again on the courthouse. The building seemed a monolith, not just of justice but of history and culture, standing testament to the many tragic tales that had unfolded within its walls.

Inside, decisions would be made that could rupture or reconcile the social fabric holding the city together. Alan was acutely aware of his role in this unfolding narrative. He had to balance his pursuit of the truth with the tenuous threads of public sentiment. As he glanced at the banners that oscillated above the crowd, he detected a telling pattern: the conflict between those rallying for a fair trial and those demanding an immediate reckoning.

It wasn't just about this case; it was about how society perceived artists and those struggling with mental health. Alan thought of the many young talents he'd seen tarnished by scandal and public disdain. The compassion for a tortured artist often tipped into dangerous empathy, while the need for justice sometimes morphed into vindictive pursuit.

He stood on the steps, feeling the tangible pressure of responsibility. From the corner of his eye, he saw the officers maintaining a defensive line. "Okay, everyone," he addressed both the officers and the crowd, his voice carrying authority and intent, "we're here to ensure justice is served. Disperse peacefully!"

Though his call may not have fully pacified the ardent demonstrators, it was enough to shift the energy just enough. The officers, visible as a unified front, kept the crowd in check. Alan could see the raw emotion in their eyes; slices of pain, defiance, and hope intermingled, forming the chaotic mosaic of public opinion.

The historical resonance of this moment wasn't wasted on Alan. The public outcry, the calls for justice, the underlying cultural friction—these were echoes of past events that had shaped the city's psyche. Mason Mind stood at the crossroads of all this tumult, his very life and legacy balanced on the knife edge of deliberation.

And so Richardson remained outside the courthouse, a sentinel against chaos, his thoughts heavy with the solemn duty to uncover the truth. Intervening to stave off unrest, he felt each protester's demand like a weight upon his shoulders, the gravity of his mission bearing down, unrelenting. As the first shouts for "Order!" began to rise, followed by several thunderous raps from the gavel, he knew the day had just begun. He was ready to unravel the intricate threads of Mason's life, one chilling revelation at a time.

A SILVER SEDAN ROLLED SMOOTHLY INTO THE VISITORS' SPACE of the federal building, its engine barely a hum before it stilled. Inside, Isaac Reynolds, his hands tightly gripping the steering wheel, sat motionless. He had been summoned from LA, from the sun-soaked boulevards and clogged freeways, back to the heart and scandal of a city shredded by serial murders. His mind pinged from one anxious thought to the next, unable to settle.

He rummaged through his briefcase, his fingers trembling as they grazed the edges of neatly stacked papers and a recorder that had captured countless interviews. The weight of his dual role as Mason's childhood friend and as a field reporter for the LA Times pressed on his chest like a stone. He checked his notes once more, memorized facts about court proceedings, and rehearsed possible questions. His eyes flicked toward the building's imposing facade, which seemed to gnaw at the morning gloom.

Isaac and Mason had been inseparable in those Long Beach days, two boys navigating a tumultuous world with art as their anchor. When Mason first confided in him about the blackouts, Isaac had dismissed them as stress-induced anomalies. That was before the incidents, before their lives warped under the weight of inexplicable violence. Those sunlit afternoons spent sketching by the shoreline felt worlds away now. How could anyone reconcile the imaginative boy who dreamed of gallery openings with the accused murderer standing trial?

He slammed the briefcase shut, a forceful punctuation to his spiraling thoughts. Each time he opened it, he dug into memories both sweet and sour, unearthing layers of complexity surrounding Mason. That last night at UCLA lingered like a stubborn stain on his consciousness. The alibi, the breakdown, the diagnosis—each fact was a pebble in Isaac's shoe, reminding him of the heavier stone he carried for Mason's innocence.

The media credentials pinned to his shirt glinted, the small placard feeling heavier by the second. He had earned his stripes chasing stories, uncovering truths cloaked in shadows, but now the stakes were personal. Shifting uncomfortably in his seat, he checked the credentials once more and then, in a moment of resolve, tucked them into his shirt. His responsibilities to the LA Times sat like a specter in the passenger seat, but for now, he needed to approach the courtroom as someone else, as Isaac Reynolds—a boy who once giggled with Mason over doodles in geometry class, over shared sandwiches, and whispered secrets.

He recalled the first art show they attended together, and the way Mason's eyes had lit up at the vivid canvases. That passion was still there, he believed, hidden beneath the layers of pain and confusion. The Quest Art Gallery wasn't just a building downtown; it was the summit of Mason's dreams, now overshadowed by grotesque accusations. Isaac's fingers traced the outline of his phone, knowing that one wrong move could annihilate their friendship, while one right move might vindicate it.

Swallowing his doubts, he drew a deep breath, attempting to shed the suffocating tension that had taken residence in his chest. The clicks of the hazard lights echoed the beats of his troubled heart.

Finally, steeling himself, Isaac unlatched the car door and stepped out. The morning air was crisp, almost biting through his tailored coat, a stark contrast to the warmth of LA. With each step towards the federal building, his mind flitted through every subtle glance Mason had ever given him, every word unspoken yet understood—each a silent plea for salvation or perhaps a confession masked by friendship.

Isaac's boots echoed hollowly on the pavement as he approached the federal steps. His shoulders squared, partly to brace against the chill and partly to summon courage, he navigated toward the main entrance, willing his resolve to remain unshaken. He knew the gravity of his presence here today, not just as a media representative but as someone who had more reasons than most to seek the real truth.

With a heavy breath and a last sweeping glance at the tumult watching from his parked sedan, Isaac ascended the steps, heading into a fortress of uncertainty and conflict, where every word and every revelation could tip the balance between salvation and damnation for the boy he once knew.

Isaac Reynolds scurried across the federal building steps, his heartbeat keeping pace with every hurried stride. The scene at the courthouse was chaotic, with police officers forming a thin blue line, attempting to control the surging crowd of protesters. Their voices rose in a chorus of anger and grievances, mingling with the shouts of reporters desperate for a shred of new information about Mason Mind.

As Isaac approached, he couldn't avoid the palpable tension in the air. Signs accusing Mason of being "The Torrential Terror" bobbed up and down, their slogans violent and accusatory. Others, smaller in number but just as vocal, demanded a fair trial, claiming systemic injustice and media bias. The public outcry was fierce, the community's fear and outrage over the unsolved serial killings boiling over, targeting Mason with a ferocity born of desperation.

Reporters, smelling a story that sold papers and airtime, circled the courthouse doors like sharks. Their questions, sharp and insistent, were flung towards anyone who paused for a moment too long. Each reporter vied to frame Mason as the face of the community's nightmare, fueling the divide between his supporters and those who saw him as a monster. The media frenzy only amplified the clamor for justice, creating a relentless pressure cooker of suspicion and fear.

Isaac, parking the silver sedan minutes earlier, now stood at the court-house, shuffling through the chaos. Noise pulsated around him, a cacophony of humanity desperate for answers, for closure. He looked skyward, words of forgiveness tangled in his mind as he neared the heavily guarded entrance. The family members of the victims, gathered mournfully at the fringe of the protest, added an emotional gravity to the tumult. Their sorrow-laden faces, pleading for accountability, intensified the stakes of this confrontation, their presence a stark reminder of the personal toll of the ongoing atrocities.

In Isaac's thoughts, the weight of his dual role pressed heavily. As

Mason's longtime friend, he'd always believed in Mason's innocence. Yet, here he stood, far from the sunny climes of their childhood, now acting as a field reporter for the LA Times, tasked with bringing the glare of public scrutiny upon his beleaguered friend.

He repeated his actions for the fourth time, nervously checking his briefcase, ensuring his notes and credentials lay where they should. The briefcase—a tether to professionalism amidst personal turmoil—was his anchor. He slipped his media credentials under his shirt, a symbolic hiding of his true intentions as he slipped through the entrance, choosing at this moment not to broadcast his affiliation but rather to seek the truth for his friend.

Isaac's mind wandered back to the information Margie had relayed to Alan Richardson earlier that day. Mason, born in 1987, was the youngest of six, a gifted artist nurtured by a scholarship to UCLA. He remembered their college days, the laughter, the struggles. The unsolved murder on campus—that haunting whisper of suspicion—never left his mind. Isaiah Long, the victim, a student with so much potential, had been found with a sedative puncture mark on her hand, her eyes removed in the most brutal of fashions. Mason's breakdown and subsequent diagnosis had always seemed like an explanation, but not to the community, never to those looking for someone to blame.

The case, sealed because Isaiah was a minor, left lingering doubts festering among those who knew Mason. How could someone so talented, so deeply troubled, fall into such a pit of suspicion? Now, years later, with bodies still being found, eyes gouged, ears severed, the connection to Mason seemed undeniable to many, a terrifying truth that they couldn't shake.

As he crossed the heavily guarded threshold, Isaac left the clamor of protest behind him. Inside, the courthouse was a stark contrast—a fortress of order amidst the external chaos. He felt the weight of the protesters' anger, the victims' families' grief, and his personal mission to find a balance between truth and friendship, fairness and justice.

Isaac stepped inside, and with a final tug at his concealed credentials, felt the world close in on him. The enormity of the situation, the proximity of law enforcement, and the silent halls of justice waiting to pass judgment all coalesced into a single pressing realization—whatever lay ahead would be the deciding factor for Mason Mind.

CHAPTER
FOUR
ACCESS GRANTED

The first light of dawn bled through the horizon, casting a golden hue on the metal sinew of the St. Louis Arch. Isaac stood for a moment, the visual splendor lost on him, his thoughts tangled in a knot of anxiety and determination. He inhaled deeply, the crisp air doing little to untangle his nerves. The stately structure before him mirrored the monumental task ahead—get through to Mason, get the truth, and somehow keep his own sanity intact.

Navigating through a sea of anxious police officers, Isaac kept his media badge tucked discreetly in his coat pocket. He knew too well that flaunting it would attract unnecessary attention and potentially jeopardize his already tenuous situation. As he maneuvered through the crowd, the weight of his impending encounter pressed heavily on his chest.

With each step, he could feel his pulse quickening. The officers' stern faces suggested they were on edge, each gaze like a mirror reflecting his own bubbling panic. He briefly locked eyes with a young cop, not much older than himself, whose eyes told a story of sleepless nights and relentless strain. Isaac wondered if his own face showed his storm of conflicted emotions—a blend of loyalty to Mason, guilt, and the chilling adrenaline of a journalist on the cusp of a career-defining story.

Clearing the mob, Isaac approached the security checkpoint. A burly officer gave him a once-over. "Media access badge," the officer grumbled, scrutinizing Isaac's outstretched hand. After a brief but nerve-wracking pause, the officer nodded, allowing him passage. Isaac's dry lips curled into a forced smile as he showed his badge, a conciliatory gesture to the halted journalists now glaring his way.

As he stepped into the building, the cool, sterile air of the federal edifice hit him. He was struck by the thought that his lifelong bond with Mason had granted him access to the belly of this beast. Yet, this realization did little to quell the rising sense of dread within him.

A kaleidoscope of thoughts assaulted Isaac's mind: Mason, the once promising artist now accused of unthinkable crimes, and the sinister figure of Hear No Evil, playing a game no one wanted to join. It all seemed too bizarre, too convoluted, to be anything but a nightmare. And yet, here Isaac was, a pawn in a lurid game threatening to overturn everything he held dear.

Isaac's internal conflict escalated with each step further into the labyrinthine corridors. His instincts screamed at the absurdity of the situation. He recalled Mason's carefree laugh and the ease with which he wielded a paintbrush, capturing worlds only visible to him. But that same Mason was now a haunted shell of a man, ensnared by inexplicable blackouts and accused of monstrosities he couldn't remember committing.

Outside, a troubled sky mirrored Isaac's inner chaos, promising another torrential downpour, as if nature itself conspired to heighten his tension. Each step felt heavier, the weight of his mission almost unbearable. He pondered his motives, ones that were not entirely pure; the tantalizing allure of a scoop that could catapult his career at LA Times shadowed his loyalty. Still, there was a genuine, desperate need to help Mason intertwine with that burgeoning professional ambition.

The officer led Isaac through checkpoints, each door a reminder of how deep into the bowels of despair his friend had descended. He wrestled with the irony of it all; the very system designed to protect was now suffocating the innocent. Or was he innocent? That lingering doubt gnawed at Isaac's resolve. The thin veneer of friendship couldn't shroud the very real possibility that Mason might be entwined with the savage acts that had the city in a chokehold.

Isaac's journey was more than physical; it was an arduous trek through the thicket of his conscience, matching pace with the palpable tension surrounding the building. Each corner turned, each blank stare exchanged with yet another officer, was a confrontation with his own misgivings. The irony wasn't lost on him; there he was, shielding his badge, when his role was to peel back layers and expose truths.

His arrival at the final checkpoint was a reluctant milestone. With a final nod from the officer, Isaac walked through the doorway, a shroud of apprehension cloaking his frame. His friendship with Mason had indeed afforded him this unique access, but at what cost? The cost was having to report back to the Mayor and Police Chief, personally. Given this access to a friend, let alone a reporter, was an unusual circumstance. But the Mayor was desperate for any information that would further this case.

His insides churned as he stepped deeper into the enigma, each step echoing louder in the silent halls, each heartbeat synching with the rhythmic quiver of the storm beginning to rouse outside.

Isaac's thoughts swirled in a vortex of memories, professional ethics, and the grim reality that awaited him. The gleaming corridors of the federal building seemed to stretch endlessly, reflecting his growing isolation. At that moment, the weight of his mission crashed over him like the thunderstorm gathering outside. He was not just stepping into a building; he was walking into a convergence of past, present, and an unpredictable future, each step drawing him closer to a revelation that would test every bond and conviction he held.

ISAAC'S HEART POUNDED IN HIS CHEST AS THE HEAVY METAL gate behind him slammed shut, each reverberation slicing through the hushed tension of the corridor. The clammy air felt suffocating, as though the very walls were closing in to smother any hope he carried within him. Every step forward echoed in the stark silence, amplifying the creeping dread that gnawed at his thoughts. He forced himself to keep moving, though each clang of the metal behind him sent a cold shiver racing down his spine.

As he ventured deeper into the bowels of the prison, Isaac's breath grew labored, his chest tightening with each passing moment. The corridors seemed too narrow, trapping him in the vice of his own anxiety. He felt sweat bead on his forehead, his pulse thrumming in his ears, drowning out any semblance of rational thought. Panic began to bloom in the pit of his stomach, spreading through his limbs like wildfire.

Trying to stave off the encroaching terror, Isaac's mind involuntarily flipped back through the pages of his childhood. He remembered the secret handshakes he and Mason concocted, their intricate rhythms a symbol of their unbreakable bond. Blood pricks sealed their loyalty, mingling crimson drops to forge a pact they thought could withstand anything. These memories flickered like the warm light of a bygone era, momentarily pushing back the shadows that threatened to engulf him.

With each breath, Isaac fought against the tightening vise grip around his chest. His vision swam, but he kept moving, propelled by a mixture of fear and determination. The muted hum of fluorescent lights buzzed above, casting a sterile glow on the grimy, cracked tiles beneath his feet. Each gate he passed through added to the oppressive weight pressing down on him, but he refused to succumb. He could almost hear Mason's voice urging him onward, a phantom echo of the childhood friend he'd once known.

Finally, the corridor opened up to the conference room, an ominous threshold that held the promise of both confrontation and reunion. Isaac's legs felt leaden, his breaths shallow and quick. The guards eyed him with a mixture of suspicion and indifference before wordlessly motioning for him to halt. They patted him down, methodically searching for contraband or hidden intentions.

Visibly distressed yet resolute, Isaac steeled himself for the encounter ahead. He needed to reassure Mason, to be the unyielding rock his friend could grasp so desperately. He had to navigate through his own fears and anxieties to reach that inner fortitude born from years of unwavering friendship. Only then could he hope to offer the solace Mason needed amidst this tempest of uncertainty and peril.

The door creaked open, revealing the cold sterility of the conference room, where everything seemed stark and uninviting. The fluorescent lights buzzed overhead, casting a harsh glare that reflected off the metal table. Isaac drew in a deep breath, his pulse finally beginning to slow. He was not here as a reporter or an outsider; he was here as a friend, and that made all the difference.

Isaac shuffled in the cold, nearly sterile conference room, the whitewashed walls closing in on him as if they were shrinking. He rearranged the few items he brought—his notebook, pen, and a cup of coffee long gone cold—his mind a tangled mess of urgency and dread. He checked his watch. The seconds seemed to stretch into infinity.

The clamor of heavy boots against the linoleum floor signaled Mason's arrival. Isaac's heart tensed with each echoing step. When the door finally opened, it wasn't the Mason he remembered who walked through. Flanked by guards, Mason appeared gaunt and beaten, his vibrant eyes now a hollow gray void. The Mason who used to throw colorful paint on canvas with wild abandon was gone, replaced by a shell of that man.

One guard leaned in, whispering to Mason, "One hour until court." Another guard fumbled with the shackles around his wrists and ankles, the metallic clicks resonating like nails in a coffin.

In the awkward silence, Isaac's breath caught in his throat, unable to form words. Instead, he clung to silent gestures—a brief nod, a twitch of his lips that failed to turn into a smile. The air between them felt heavy, laden with unspoken fears and the weight of their situation.

He glanced at his friend. Mason's shoulders drooped, his face etched with exhaustion and something closer to resignation. Their eyes met for a brief moment—a lifeless stare from Mason that sent a chill down Isaac's spine. Through that despairing gaze, a silent plea for rescue. It was a look that spoke volumes of what Mason had endured—sleepless nights, countless interrogations, a gnawing uncertainty about his own actions.

Isaac's internal battle was scarred with guilt and helplessness. A part of him questioned his motives for being here—was he acting out of duty as a reporter or out of an unyielding love for his friend? Their time shared, their immutable bond now seemed shadowed by the darkness that loomed over Mason's future.

In the stillness, Isaac remembered the day Mason lost his parents in a car accident. They were barely teenagers. Isaac had sat with Mason in his room, surrounded by unfinished sketches and paint tubes. They didn't say much—there were no words for grief of that magnitude—but their silent company spoke louder than any consolation. That innate understanding was what Isaac clung to now.

He wished there was something—anything—he could say or do to lift some of the burden off Mason's shoulders. The guard's watchful eyes reminded him of his limitations. The institutional coldness of the room seemed to amplify their isolation. He wished he could reach across the table, touch Mason's hand, and tell him that he believed in him and that they would get through this together.

Every so often, Mason would lift his head slightly, his gaze flickering around the room as if searching for an escape. Isaac noticed small details— a light sheen of perspiration on Mason's forehead, the twitching of his fingers, the slow, deliberate blinks.

The room continued to close in, the silence almost unbearable. Isaac shifted in his chair, feigned adjusting his accessories, though they were already perfectly aligned. The gesture was more to distract himself from the suffocating stillness and the profound sense of loss radiating off Mason.

Without words, Isaac conveyed a promise—one forged from years of unspoken trust and understanding. Despite the shadows darkening their path, despite the chilling silence that shrouded them, he silently vowed to stand by his friend, just as he had in their youth. Their eyes locked again, if only briefly, and in that flicker of connection, a shimmer of hope, however faint, bloomed.

ISAAC AND MASON SAT IN THE CONFERENCE ROOM, SILENCE stretching between them like a taut wire. The rain tapped insistently against the windowsill, each drop distinct yet melding into a relentless symphony. Isaac's eyes darted to Mason, who seemed a shadow of his former self, his once vibrant spirit now dulled and frayed. Mason's fingers trembled atop the cold metal table, a stark contrast to the stillness of his slumped form, his head hanging low.

The storm outside intensified, and Mason's posture stiffened. He jerked to his feet with startling abruptness, moving toward the window as the sky cracked open with a fierce thunderous roar. Isaac's heart clenched watching his friend struggle, every clap of thunder seemingly a physical blow to Mason's psyche.

"I hate the rain," Mason spat out, his voice filled with a raw, guttural intensity. Beads of sweat slid down his forehead, tracing lines of his invisible torment. He wiped his brow with the back of his hand, his breaths shallow and quick. Every gust of wind, each flicker of lightning, seemed to drag Mason deeper into a past he couldn't escape, a memory he could never forget.

Isaac, sensing Mason's unraveling, reached into his pocket and discreetly activated his tape recorder. He had to document this, not for the headlines but because understanding Mason's trauma might be the only way to clear his name.

The words tumbled from Mason in a cascade. "I was just a kid," he began, eyes unfocused as if seeing a scene far removed from this sterile room. "The rain was just like this—heavy, unyielding. I remember the sound of it smothering everything around me, and then... the scream. It cut through the storm. I hid behind a tree, watching as a boy... oh God, he... he removed her eyes out of their sockets in the alley."

Mason's legs buckled, and he leaned heavily against the window frame, knuckles white from gripping the sill. The rain continued its relentless patter, mingling with the echoes of his horror-stricken voice as it painted a odious portrait of his childhood memory.

Mason's face contorted in anguish. "Every storm since then... it's like being back in that moment. My mind shuts off... I can't breathe; I just... I can't escape it."

Isaac edged closer, his voice low and filled with concern. "You're not alone, Mason. You don't have to face this alone."

Mason spun around, eyes wild and glassy. "But what if... What if they're right? What if the blackout is just an excuse, just a cover for something monstrous inside me?"

Isaac's grip tightened around the tape recorder, his heart a jumble of loyalty and dread. He struggled with his own fears and the gnawing questions about his friend's innocence. Still, this wasn't about headlines anymore; it was about empathy, understanding, and the bond they shared.

"You're not a monster, Mason," Isaac stated firmly, stepping closer to his friend. "You can't be. I know the person you are—the artist, the dreamer. There's no way you could become this... this Torrential Terror."

Mason's eyes searched Isaac's face, seeking solace yet finding only more questions. His breath hitched in his throat as the wind howled outside, rattling the window panes. "I don't even remember half the things they're accusing me of. How do I fight something I can't even recall?"

Isaac placed a reassuring hand on Mason's arm. "We will find the truth. Together. But you have to trust in that and in yourself."

Mason's shoulders sagged, the weight of years of torment and the present uncertainty pressing down on him. The storm outside mirrored the turmoil within the room, every crash of thunder like a punctuation mark to Mason's revelations. For a moment, just a brief heartbeat, there was a glimmer of hope in Mason's eyes, quickly overshadowed by the dark clouds of his doubt and fear.

Isaac knew that every step forward would be fraught with challenges, not only in proving Mason's innocence but also in helping him reclaim fragments of his shattered psyche. The task was becoming portentous, like the storm raging beyond their reach—wild, unpredictable, and perilous. Yet within that chaos was the unyielding flicker of their friendship, a beacon in their darkest hour.

Isaac and Mason faced each other across the cold, metal table, the air thick with unspoken words and unshed tears. The room was a sterile cage, the walls seemingly closing in as the raw scent of fear and distrust grew between them. Isaac's knuckles whitened as he clenched his fists beneath the table, desperately trying to keep his voice steady.

"I don't believe you're guilty, Mason," Isaac said, his voice a strained whisper. Each word felt like it teetered on the brink of shattering an already delicate balance. The sound of the rain drumming on the windows was relentless, a haunting echo amplifying the tension.

Mason's eyes, usually so vibrant with creativity, now seemed hollow and distant. He tilted his head slightly, scrutinizing Isaac with a mix of suspicion and hurt. "Is that what you're here to say? To protect your byline?" Mason's voice was eerily calm, a stark contrast to the storm raging outside.

Isaac flinched as if struck. His mind raced back to their shared childhood memories. Now, it felt fragile, like a paper boat in a tempest.

"My uncle told me about your new job at the LA Times," Mason continued, his eyes narrowing. "Didn't think to mention it, did you?" The accusation dripped with bitterness, each word a barb meant to wound.

An icy emptiness pooled in Isaac's stomach. The room seemed to blur slightly, the fluorescent lights casting shadows that danced mockingly. "What? My job... has nothing to do with this," he stammered, trying to process the sudden shift in conversation.

Mason leaned forward, the movement jolting Isaac back to the harsh reality of the moment. "Doesn't it? My uncle said you'd been digging into my case, looking for a scoop. Are you here as my friend or as a reporter?"

The blow landed harder than any physical strike could have. Isaac's world tilted, confusion and anger intertwining. "You think I would sell you out, Mason? After everything?" His voice trembled, rage mixing with the sting of betrayal.

Mason's pupils dilated, his breath quickening. "Why wouldn't you? Everyone else has."

Isaac felt a fire ignite in his chest, burning away the last vestiges of restraint. "I came here to help you, not to ruin you! I've dedicated my life to journalism—to uncovering the truth! But you—" He broke off, shaking his head as regret swamped his features.

The storm outside clashed with the storm within. The truth of Mason's words collided with Isaac's denial, both twisting the knife deeper into their shared history. The affable boy who once shared secrets by flashlight now stared at him like a stranger.

The silence was deafening, broken only by the rain's relentless hiss. A single tear slid down Mason's cheek, unnoticed and unacknowledged. Isaac's anger melted into choking, bone-deep sorrow. He stood, walked around the table, and knelt beside the shell of his friend.

"I'm sorry," he said, the words cracking with genuine regret. "I was wrong. I swear to you, I'll report the truth. For you. For us."

Mason looked at him with an expression caught between despair and the faint glimmer of hope. "Is there any truth left to tell?"

Isaac placed a hand on Mason's shoulder, hoping to convey the depth of his sincerity. "We'll find it together. I promise."

The room, though unchanged, felt slightly less suffocating. Isaac helped Mason to his feet, their shared history a fragile lifeline in a turbulent sea. The storm outside continued its symphony, but now it was merely background noise to the unspoken vow of truth and redemption that remained between them.

Isaac leaned in, his eyes connecting with Mason's. "I'm here for you," he whispered, his voice a tremble of sincerity. "Whatever it takes, I'll make sure your story gets out. The truth, no distortions."

Mason's lips curled into a wry smile, his eyes hollow, a reflection of the torment embedded in his soul. "The media doesn't care about the truth, Isaac. They want headlines. They want blood." Laughter thick with bitterness followed his words. It echoed against the dreary walls of the conference room, a room that seemed as void of hope as Mason's eyes.

Isaac flinched but didn't recoil. He steadied himself and moved closer, the slight creak of his chair cutting through the tension. "Maybe most of them don't," he admitted, his voice firmer now, "but I do. I've got integrity, Mason. And I've got you."

Mason turned away, his eyes tracing the barred window, through which a fleeting glimpse of sunlight wrestled with encroaching storm clouds. "How can I believe that?" Mason's low and raw voice broke the silence. "How can I trust any of this... or even myself?"

Isaac's heart clenched at the sight of his friend's desolation. He inched closer, his presence a beckon of steadfast loyalty. "Remember why we became friends in the first place? We trusted each other, no matter what. You're not alone in this, Mason." His voice caught, laden with the earnest commitment of a childhood promise morphing into an adult vow.

Mason's eyes met Isaac's again, the spark of long-buried trust kindling slowly. "It's hard to remember those times when all I see are the nightmares," Mason confessed, his voice softening.

Isaac nodded, his throat tight. He retrieved his tape recorder and set it on the table, a gentle click punctuating the air. "Start from the beginning. Every detail, no holds barred. Let's untangle this together."

With a resignation sigh, Mason began. "It all started on that stormy night when I was a child." His voice quivered slightly as it flowed, each word an admission. "I saw something I wasn't supposed to. Blood, chaos, and... those eyes, those empty, accusing eyes."

Isaac's pen scratched feverishly, capturing each fragment of Mason's fragmented past. He listened intently, the ink etching a tale of terror and confusion. This was more than a story; this was Mason's salvation.

Mason paused, the intensity of the memories overwhelming him. He clutched his hands together, the knuckles white from the strain. "I'm scared, Isaac. Scared of what I might be capable of during those blackouts. Scared that the person in those headlines is... me."

Isaac's gaze hardened with determination. "You aren't that person," he stated emphatically. "We'll find the truth. You must believe that."

"Okay," Mason said finally, his voice barely more than a whisper. "Okay, let's do this."

The storm clouds outside seemed to gather ominously, as if the sky itself were bracing for the tale about to be told. This moment marked a turning point in their lives—a rekindled trust forged stronger in the face of the emerging storm. With each word Mason spoke, the conspiracy of silence surrounding his memories began to unravel, piece by piece.

Isaac leaned in closer, absorbing the gravity of Mason's revelations. The air grew thicker, charged with an unspoken promise. Sensationalism could never capture the raw truth spilling between them now. Isaac's resolve crystallized: he would document every word, every detail. This story was far more than an article. It was a lifeline for his friend, a lifeline he intended to hold onto, no matter how tumultuous the journey ahead.

Mason took a deep breath and continued, his voice steadier now. The room, suffused with the weight of unvoiced fears and newfound hope, bore silent witness to their commitment to truth, a flicker of resilience lighting the shadows. The steel door creaked back open, and two guards walked in. One guard stood back dangling the shackles in his hand while the other approached the table with an empathic voice, "It's time for court."

CHAPTER
FIVE
HEAR NO EVIL

The early Monday morning air in the downtown St. Louis Police Department headquarters crackled with urgency. Phones rang incessantly, like a chorus of alarms, and officers hustled back and forth, their footsteps echoing off the cold, tiled floors. It was chaotic, each officer battling the incessant demands of paperwork, phone calls, and the relentless surge of activity that seemed to define the start of each new week.

Sgt. Henderson stood at the center of it all, firmly rooted amidst the whirlwind, barking orders with the authority that years of experience had afforded him. His sharp and discerning eyes scanned the room, missing nothing. He shouted, "Officer Miller and Officer Torres, you stay," he continued. "I heard about the motorcycle pursuit over on 10th St. I also heard that he got away after going down a dead-end street."

Both officers stood still as statues, cleared their throats, and looked away in shame. "What that tells me is that you two are not learning your district and are depending on GPS too much," his voice cutting through the clamor like a knife through a cloth.

"Post-explosion protocol deployment! Secure the courthouse steps, now!" His tone left no room for hesitation, but then it hardened, a dry reprimand: "And for God's sake, stop relying on that GPS! Use your heads, won't you?"

For all his sternness, there was an undercurrent of paternal concern in Sgt. Henderson's demeanor. The younger officers respected him, partly out of fear and mostly out of a deep-rooted recognition of his dedication to their safety and growth. His authority was tempered by an unspoken commitment to mentoring, ensuring that, while he demanded much, he also gave just as much back in guidance.

Outside, the sound of screeching tires announced the arrival of Jason Fall, a young UPS driver renowned for his reckless speed and equally infectious charisma. His truck, adorned with the company's brown insignia, came to an abrupt halt, and Jason hopped out, the melody of a rock song still blaring from the truck's speakers. The officers nearest to him broke into laughter and song, their voices weaving into a jovial greeting that momentarily lightened the day's heavy atmosphere.

"Paulie! You ever think of joining the band?" One officer teased, slapping Jason on the back with a hearty welcome.

Jason returned the gesture with a high-five, laughing. His relationship with the department was not just about deliveries; it was steeped in camaraderie. From the playful ribbing about his questionable driving skills to shared laughter over past mishaps—like the time he'd delivered a package to Lt. Rozzoro's house and accidentally triggered her home alarm—the connection ran deep, fortified by mutual respect and a shared sense of community.

As Jason retrieved the package for the St. Louis Police Department headquarters from the back of his truck, today felt no different. The package was nondescript, wrapped securely in brown paper, and bound with robust packing tape. He made his way to the front desk, where Sgt. Henderson was still giving a stern lecture to Officers Miller and Torres.

Jason waited patiently, leaning casually against the desk. He watched Sgt. Henderson with an amused expression, not unfamiliar with the sergeant's no-nonsense attitude. Finally, Sgt. Henderson's attention shifted to him.

"Morning, Jason. What's the future lawyer of St. Louis got for us today?" Sgt. Henderson inquired, his tone a rare mix of casual ease and genuine interest.

Jason grinned, "Just the usual. And hey, I'm sticking with political science; you never know, I might be your boss someday."

The sergeant chuckled, a rare sound that softened his stern exterior. "Aim high, kid. You've got the chops for it."

With a nod of approval, Sgt. Henderson reached for the package and placed it on his desk. A seemingly mundane routine that masked the unseen horror waiting to be unveiled. The bond between Jason and the officers, the blend of levity amidst their morning duties, painted a picture of normalcy—a delicate balance poised on the edge of shattering reality. The police officers, though often hardened by the somberness of their duties, found respite in these fleeting moments of camaraderie, where laughter punctuated the seriousness of their world.

Meanwhile, Sgt. Henderson placed the package on his desk, the simple action underscored by a nagging unease he couldn't quite place. The morning's lively banter gave way to a more somber mood, the weight of the package settling like a stone in the collective gut of the room. Each member of the station knew too well the thin line separating daily routine from the dark undercurrents that could, at any moment, pull them into the abyss.

The officers carried on, their movements slower and more deliberate, as if subconsciously bracing for the impact of whatever lay ahead. The lobby's previous chorus of ringing phones and hurried steps had dulled to a steady hum, the anticipatory silence creeping in.

And within that package, the grotesque reality awaited—a daunting testament to the insidious evil lurking in the shadows, biding its time to unleash horror upon the unsuspecting. This moment of unity and banter was but a fragile veneer, soon to be torn asunder by the darkness breathing life behind the ordinary brown paper.

Yet, for now, the lobby held onto its semblance of normalcy, unaware of the storm that was about to descend upon them, the heinous contents of the package a ticking time bomb of dread and chaos, ready to rupture the fabric of their day.

SGT. HENDERSON'S HANDS TREMBLED SLIGHTLY AS HE GRIPPED his silver Army pocketknife, the weight of responsibility gnawing at his insides. As he slid the blade into the tape, his lungs tightened with a mixture of dread and reluctance. The recent demands and threats from Hear No Evil clouded his mind like a storm. Every sinew in his body tensed as he sliced the tape with a swift WHOOP, memories of past horrors playing like a reprehensible slideshow in his thoughts.

With the tape cracked open, Sgt. Henderson's eyes widened as he flipped back the flaps of the package. The grotesque contents slowly revealed themselves, appearing like a nightmarish bloom. A severed head sat staring up at him, the ears vacant and haunting in their emptiness. He staggered back, stool rattling and toppling behind him. His breath caught in his throat, the image burning into his core.

Jason's curiosity had morphed into an anxious tremor, pulling him to the box against the silent pleas in Sgt. Henderson's eyes. Hesitation warred with a desperate, instinctual pull towards the unknown. The air thickened around him as he stepped closer, heart pounding, chest tight with each tentative breath. Sgt. Henderson's outstretched arms, meant to block the driver's view, barely registered as Jason peered over the top of the package.

A scream pierced the charged atmosphere, raw and primal, severing any veil of safety. Jason stumbled back, his face blanching upon the sight of the severed head. The reality of the disfigured human remains crashed upon him, drowning him in sheer panic. His legs launched into flight before his mind could catch up, self-preservation kicking in hard. His headphones slipped from his grasp, falling to the ground with a clatter as he bolted from the police station, breath ragged with terror.

Officers reached to restrain him, but Jason, in a panic, waved them off and stumbled back into his truck. As he drove away, the tires screeching as the melody of his outgoing music lingered in the air, a brief echo of terror that starkly contrasted with the ominous uncertainty that loomed on the horizon.

Sgt. Henderson remained a refuge amidst the chaos, forcing himself to piece together fragments of his resolve. He kneeled to retrieve Jason's fallen headphones, an almost reflexive act in his state of shock. Carefully placing them on the shelf behind his desk, he took a moment to steady his shaking hands, trying to anchor himself from the spiraling madness. The image of the severed head lingered, a threatening reminder of the grim task that lay ahead.

SGT. HENDERSON'S HANDS TREMBLED SLIGHTLY AS HE LOOKED into the box again, half-expecting its contents to transform into something less horrific. But the grim reality stood steadfast: a severed head, devoid of ears, lay nestled among the packing peanuts like a revolting relic of human cruelty. He felt the bile rising in his throat but swallowed it down, forcing himself to maintain a semblance of composure. He closed the box as carefully as he could, the lid making a dull thud that echoed ominously in the lobby.

Dialing the number to the police commissioner's office, Sgt. Henderson wiped the sweat from his brow. Each ring on the line felt like an eternity, a pulse of dread in sync with his racing heart. The chaos in the station buzzed around him—officers barking orders, phones incessantly shrilling, the distinct clatter of hurried footsteps. Desperation clung to the air like the city's lingering humidity after a heavy rainstorm.

"This is Sgt. Henderson. I need to speak with the Chief. It's urgent," he managed to say, struggling to keep his voice steady.

The line held for a moment, then crackled as it was transferred. The city's weight bore down on him, intensified by the relentless media circus and the chilling whispers of paranoia threading through the alleys and homes. St. Louis hadn't been the same ever since Hear No Evil and The Torrential Terror began their reigns of terror. Citizens moved with wary eyes, their steps quickened by unseen fears. The media latched onto every rumor, every despicable detail, further fraying the collective nerves of the population.

"The Chief here," came the stern voice through the receiver.

"Sir, we... we received a package," Sgt. Henderson began, forcing the words through the tightness in his throat. "Inside was a severed head. No ears. There was a letter from Hear No Evil. He demands Mason Mind's release immediately."

Silence lingered heavily for a moment, the kind that makes even the smallest sounds—like the scurrying of an officer dropping a stack of files— seem deafening. Sgt. Henderson's pulse thrummed in his ears, a constant reminder of his insurmountable duty.

"Read the letter," the Chief's voice commanded, terse and thick with concern.

Sgt. Henderson unfolded the letter, his eyes scanning the jagged script that looked like it was penned by the devil himself. It read:

Release Mason Mind. Fail, and the streets will soak with twice the blood. The countdown starts now.

As he relayed the words to the Chief, Sgt. Henderson could feel the atmosphere in the room shift. The officers around him, those who had overheard, seemed to move with a new severity, their faces grim and drawn. A casual camaraderie that had barely held the desperation at bay now vanished, replaced by the deadly seriousness of their escalating war against a phantom enemy.

"This is unprecedented," the Chief finally uttered, a mixture of frustration and dread coating his words. "We can't give in to terrorist demands, but if we don't... the consequences," his voice trailed off, leaving the rest unsaid. History whispered its tragedies—times when the city had faced evil and faltered, leaving scars on its collective memory.

"We need options, strategies," Sgt. Henderson pressed. "Before word gets out, before people lose the last scraps of faith they have in us."

The Chief's pause felt heavy with contemplation. The entire city's gaze seemed to zero in on this fragile moment, balanced on the precipice of chaos. Law enforcement was strained to its limits as officers worked double shifts and traded personal lives for the never-ending pursuit of two ghosts haunting their city with nightmarish precision. Any mistake now would not merely be a blot on careers; it would translate into lost lives, shattered families, and another tally on a killer's scorecard.

"Stay put," the Chief finally instructed. "I'm sending Alan Richardson down to you. We need the Nightwalker on this. Keep the area secured; no leaks to the media. This must stay contained until we have a plan."

Sgt. Henderson merely nodded, even though the Chief couldn't see him. In his mind, he imagined the whispered conversations spreading like wildfire through the city, each word a spark threatening to ignite the volatile air of public trust—or what little remained of it. As he hung up the phone, he took a deep breath, his hand still hovering close to the receiver as if reluctant to sever the connection to someone else sharing the weight of the crisis.

The reality sank deeper; the battle lines were drawn not only against a visible enemy but also against the creeping dread that threatened to tear the city apart from within. The fight was on every front—in the dusty corners of police precincts, in the anxious glances of neighbors, and, most pressingly, in the remaining hours gifted by a murderous ultimatum.

Sgt. Henderson glanced down at the now-closed box, its evil contained but ever-present. He steeled himself, understanding fully the gravity of Hear No Evil's twisted message. Every heartbeat, every errant thought could be their undoing. As the Chief's words settled, he knew they were at a dire crossroads where decisions bore the weight of countless lives, and only precision and bravery would see them through to dawn.

CHAPTER

SIX

FORENSIC

Lieutenant Lisa Rozzoro's heels echoed through the sterile corridors of the St. Louis Police Department headquarters as the day's early light filtered through the frosted windows, casting a cold, clinical glow. She approached the front lobby desk with a spark of enthusiasm radiating from her lithe figure, her eyes alive with a sense of purpose.

Sgt. Henderson looked up from his paperwork, his brow furrowing as he noticed her approach. This stint at the front desk had given him a different kind of appreciation for the methodical nature of the job—keeping the growing tension of the city's crime-ridden streets at bay, if only momentarily. He noted Lt. Rozzoro's buoyant energy, a stark contrast to the pervading gloom that had settled over the department like a heavy mist.

"Good morning, Sgt. Henderson," Lt. Rozzoro began, her voice tinged with excitement. "Today's the big day! We have ten of the brightest high school students visiting our new forensic lab."

Sgt. Henderson's expression tightened, a flicker of concern passing across his face. The department had been on high alert, with two active serial killers leaving everyone on edge. The recent opening of the forensic lab had been a glimmer of hope in an otherwise grim landscape. State-of-the-art technology tamed the unknown, deciphering clues from chaos—a beacon akin to a lighthouse cutting through an impenetrable fog.

"The kids are visiting today?" Sgt. Henderson asked, his tone skeptical. "With everything going on, is that such a good idea?"

Lt. Rozzoro gave a reassuring smile, though the underlying edge in her eyes betrayed the gravity of her thoughts. "I've planned everything meticulously. Their visit is going to be safe and well-timed, I promise. It's vital for them to see how the lab can help solve crimes, especially with the recent cases."

Sgt. Henderson shook his head slightly. "You know I trust your judgment, Lt. Rozzoro, but these killers—Hear No Evil and Torrential Terror —have everyone on edge. We can't afford to take risks."

The mention of the killers brought an additional weight to the air, tangible and oppressive. As if the actions of Hear No Evil had not caused enough gloom and despair; there was the added stress caused by the Torrential Terror, also referred to as The Enucleator, because their victims' eyeballs had been removed, multiplying the threat and shadowing the city in newfound terror. Solving these cases required traditional detective work and the innovative forensics that the new lab promised. Leveraging advanced DNA analysis, digital forensics, and real-time crime scene recreations, the lab stood as a frontier of justice.

Lt. Rozzoro nodded, empathy threading through her professional demeanor. "I understand your concern, Sgt. Henderson. Still, showcasing our new lab is crucial for restoring public confidence. Plus, these kids— they're the future. Inspiring them now could mean fewer mistakes and more advanced methods as they enter the field."

Sgt. Henderson's eyes softened slightly, the fatherly part of him appreciating her sentiment. "Alright, Lt. Rozzoro. We'll keep it tight. Just make sure they're in and out without any hiccups."

As they conversed, the front lobby's mood seemed to shift. The walls themselves, historical sentinels of countless confessions and breakdowns, seemed to listen in, absorbing the palpable sense of duty that governed the precinct. The presence of young, optimistic minds within the heavy, somber heart of police operations seemed almost a juxtaposing hope against the backdrop of recurring nightmares.

The police department had longed for a new forensic lab. Its establishment was a testimony to modern ingenuity meeting the primal need for order and justice. Its establishment was timely, especially as the city's crime statistics had painted a grim picture over the years. The advent of the two new serial killers had pushed the community to demand actionable solutions, and the lab's advanced capabilities were a direct answer. They promised efficiency and, most critically, an unerring eye toward justice. Where once there had been doubt and wrongful accusations, there would now be solid evidence and undeniable facts.

What spurred this significant leap in capability was not just technological advancement but a pledge to improve the justice system's integrity. The specter of Mason Mind, an inspiring artist caught in the turmoil of his blackouts and wrongful accusations, was overshadowing. Mason's predicament illustrated the forensic lab's potential to save innocents from the jaws of mistaken guilt, elevating evidence to an almost sacrosanct level within the city's judicial process.

With a collective breath, Lt. Rozzoro and Sgt. Henderson fell silent, the weight of their responsibilities pressing down on them. They both knew that today's visit was not just a simple educational trip; it was symbolic. It was a statement of resilience and unwavering dedication to enlightening young minds amidst adversity. Though the city's shadows grew longer with each crime, streaks of light still pierced through, promising clarity, promising truth.

With a final nod, Lt. Lisa Rozzoro turned on her heel, her footsteps now solemn in purpose. Sgt. Henderson watched her go, a reluctant yet hopeful resolve settling in his chest. The safety and timing of this visit were now bound by their unspoken commitment to better days, to justice, and the future.

A SHORT YELLOW BUS PULLED IN FRONT OF THE POLICE headquarters, its flashing lights bouncing off the building's imposing façade. The dawn cast long shadows, juxtaposed against the unwavering beams of the bus's lights. The first light of day barely penetrated the pervasive gloom that seemed to be a constant companion to the city—a city entrapped in the clutches of chilling serial murders.

Ms. Ann, stepping off the bus with practiced authority, motioned for the students to follow. Each student exited the bus in a single file, their faces a mixture of somber curiosity and nervous excitement. They didn't yet realize they were stepping into a place where each corner harbored stories of unspeakable horror and silent heroism.

Lt. Rozzoro, standing by the entrance, exuded infectious enthusiasm. Her uniform pristine and her posture proud, she aimed to be a beacon of positivity amidst the surrounding tension. The faint hum of police radios and distant sounds from the streets underscored the gravity of her occupation. As the children approached, she greeted them with a broad and warm smile.

"Welcome, junior detectives!" she greeted, her voice melodic with excitement. "Today, you embark on a journey that will not only be thrilling but deeply impactful. Your participation in the youth cadet law enforcement program isn't just about visiting our headquarters—it's about understanding the real impact you can have in our community."

Her eyes sparkled as she spoke, recalling the day her own path toward law enforcement had unfolded before her feet. "When I was your age," she began, ensuring she had their undivided attention. "I was inspired by those who protected and served. Today, I hope to pass that inspiration on to you."

The students listened intently, some returning her smiles shyly, while others beamed with eager anticipation. The chilling undertone of the city, where unsolved mysteries lingered like phantoms in the shadows, was momentarily forgotten in the light of Lt. Rozzoro's captivating presence.

Inside the headquarters, the atmosphere transformed from external gloom to an intriguing maze of bustling activity and purpose. Lt. Rozzoro's voice resonated against the walls, guiding the students through the day's schedule with an energy that seemed to defy the building's normally grave aura. She animatedly described the upcoming sessions—a tour of the forensic labs, hands-on fingerprinting activities, and a special lesson on crime scene investigations. Her words were designed to captivate their young minds, to implant the seeds of curiosity and civic duty.

"Every action you take today, no matter how small it may seem, can contribute to solving big mysteries," she encouraged, her voice firm and motivating. "You have the power to change lives, starting with your own."

One of the students, a boy named Ralph, couldn't contain his enthusiasm. "Lieutenant, will we get to see how real detectives work?" He asked, his voice cracking slightly with excitement.

Lt. Rozzoro nodded affirmatively, her eyes brimming with pride and hope. "Absolutely, Ralph. You'll not only see what we do, but you'll also get to participate in some of the processes. Each of you has the potential to become a vital part of our community's future."

Their interactions filled the space with a temporary lightness, a stark contrast to the heavy burdens carried by the officers and detectives who walked these halls daily. The program, Lt. Rozzoro believed, was a crucial step in bridging the gap between the police and the community. Each child here deserved to know that they played a significant role in a collective future.

As they moved deeper into the headquarters, Lt. Rozzoro maintained her engaging demeanor, pausing often to ensure every student felt included. She wasn't merely an officer to them; she was a mentor, a guide steering them through the murky waters of the adult world, all the while shielding them from its most brutal truths.

Leading them inside with the careful hand of a guardian, Lt. Rozzoro demonstrated how the building functioned like a living organism with every heartbeat—a phone ringing, an officer briefing, a detective deep in thought—contributing to the fight against those who sought to spread terror. She wanted these children to understand the mechanics of law enforcement while additionally understanding the heart and soul that drove men and women who donned the uniform daily and faced the encroaching darkness without flinching.

As they congregated in the main lobby, Lt. Rozzoro ensured the final moments before they split to their next destinations were filled with encouragement and anticipation. "Remember," she said, looking at each one of them with unwavering resolve. "Today you start a journey that will allow you to make real differences. Stay curious, be brave, and always remember that together we can bring light to the darkest places."

With that, Lt. Rozzoro guided the students deeper into the building, her voice and presence a shield against the lurking shadows, instilling a sense that they too could be harbingers of justice in a world fraught with unseen dangers.

Lieutenant Lisa Rozzoro guided the eager group of high school students through the maze-like halls of the St. Louis Police

Department headquarters. The scent of freshly painted walls mingled with the faint tang of disinfectant, giving the place an unsettling balance of newness and sterility. The students, clad in their neat uniforms, followed Lt. Rozzoro with wide-eyed curiosity, their footsteps echoing off the polished floors.

They entered a spacious classroom, its sterile ambiance contrasting with their vibrant energy. Lt. Rozzoro's eyes sparkled with a blend of excitement and authority as she motioned for the students to place their belongings on the desks. They did so, shuffling nervously before standing beside their assigned spots with small puffs of anxious breath hanging in the cold air.

The ceremonial aspect of their induction began to settle over them like a heavy fog. The reality of being sworn in as junior detectives evolved from a distant dream. They were no longer just students on a field trip; they were stepping into the shoes of city protectors, and the gravity of this shift weighed on their young shoulders.

Lt. Rozzoro stood at the head of the room, her posture straight and commanding under the stark fluorescent lights. She raised her hand and called for the room's attention, her voice clear and authoritative. "Ladies and gentlemen, today marks the beginning of your introduction to the world of law enforcement. As junior detectives, you will witness firsthand the duties and responsibilities that come with wearing a badge."

The students' excitement intermingled with a creeping uncertainty. Some exchanged glances, their faces flushed with a mixture of pride and apprehension. For many, this was their first encounter with the profound seriousness that underpinned their newfound roles. The prospect of contributing to the fight against the town's recent surge of serial killings tugged at their consciousness, sharpening their sense of purpose.

Lt. Rozzoro continued, her words wrapping around the students like a binding cord. "You will be sworn in shortly. With that oath comes a commitment to uphold the values we cherish—integrity, courage, and dedication. Our city battles an unseen yet malevolent force; your part, though small, carries immense significance."

As the formal ceremony began, the students stiffened, their eyes gleaming with anticipation. Hands trembled slightly as they were instructed to raise them for the oath. Repeating the solemn words after the lieutenant, a profound sense of duty began to course through their veins.

Each phrase they echoed seemed to etch responsibility deeper into their hearts.

Lt. Rozzoro paced in front of them, her gaze piercing theirs with each step. "Remember, the path you embark on today is laden with challenges. Our goal is not just to catch criminals but to understand and prevent crimes before they happen. Your training will cover various aspects, including forensic science, investigative techniques, and public safety protocols."

As she spoke, the students' minds buzzed with thoughts, their youthful imaginations running wild with visions of solving the town's most horrendous mysteries. The sinister whispers of serial killers like Torrential Terror and Hear No Evil fluttered at the edge of their thoughts, turning momentary flashes of excitement into sober reflection.

The class interaction came to a close with Lt. Rozzoro instructing the newly sworn junior detectives to discuss the day's activities and training. This marked the beginning of their rigorous journey. Each student's internal dialogue echoed with the determination to prove themselves capable, to be more than just passive observers in a city gripped by fear.

Lt. Rozzoro's words played over in their heads as they contemplated the weight of their roles. The gravity of the city's current situation—haunted by the Torrential Terror and Hear No Evil—cast a shadow over their enthusiasm. But within that shadow, each student felt a flicker of resolve. They imagined the lives lost to these killers, and it lit a fire, a fervent determination to be part of the solution.

As Lt. Rozzoro dismissed the class, the students fell into hushed conversations about what lay ahead. The earlier exuberance was tempered by the somber reality of their new roles. They exited the classroom, eager to embark on the next phase of their journey in the fingerprint lab, ready to dive into the meticulous world of forensic science.

With each step, nervous anticipation gave way to burgeoning confidence. Their collective aim—a shared purpose to aid in the relentless pursuit of justice—grew stronger, intertwining their fates with the storied legacy of the St. Louis Police Department's resolve against its worst fears.

LT. ROZZORO LED THE GROUP OF JUNIOR DETECTIVES INTO THE fingerprint lab, her movements brisk and purposeful. The sterile environment buzzed with quiet activity, the hum of equipment mingling with the faint smell of antiseptic. Sterilized white walls contrasted against the white countertops strewn with forensic tools, embodying the essence of scientific rigor.

"Welcome to the fingerprint lab," Lt. Rozzoro began, her voice clear and commanding. "Here, we gather one of the most crucial pieces of evidence in crime investigations—fingerprints." She gestured to the students to form a semicircle around her as she started her lesson.

Fingerprints, she explained, are the unique, unchanging patterns found on the tips of our fingers, created by the sweat glands beneath the skin. Each loop, whorl, and arch tells a story, capturing a moment in time and space. It was a revolutionary advancement in the late 19th century when Sir Francis Galton and Sir Henry Faulds independently studied and classified fingerprints, eventually leading to the identification of individuals through these intricate patterns.

"The importance of maintaining professionalism with each sample cannot be overstated," Lt. Rozzoro continued, emphasizing her point by holding up a pair of rubber gloves. "Contamination compromises evidence, leading to potential misidentifications and jeopardizing entire cases." She scanned the eager faces before her, hoping her gravity resonated with them. This wasn't merely a science lesson; it was about preserving justice.

As Lt. Rozzoro demonstrated how to gently dust a fingerprint sample with magnetic powder and lift it using collection tape, her thoughts wandered to the impact of fingerprinting technology on modern crime scene investigations. The transition from ink pads and manual classification to computerized databases had not only increased efficiency but also cemented fingerprints as irrefutable evidence in courts. Their reliability could exonerate the innocent and condemn the guilty, making the stakes unbelievably high for everyone involved.

"Does anyone know why fingerprints are distinctive?" she asked, glancing around the room. One student, a bespectacled boy with a mop of curly hair, raised his hand. "Because no two people have the same fingerprints, not even twins!"

"Exactly," she affirmed. "In a world where physical appearances can deceive, fingerprints offer a unique identifier that science can trust."

However, she noted privately, the growing reliance on fingerprint databases also brought about concerns regarding privacy and the potential for wrongful accusations. People trusted forensic science, but the implications of a mistake could be devastating, affecting lives and invoking widespread doubt over the justice system.

Noticing the preprocessed samples were now complete, she instructed, "I need a volunteer to fetch an unprocessed item from Sgt. Henderson at the front desk." A hand shot up—Ralph Henry, a bright-eyed and enthusiastic student, eager to prove himself.

"Ralph, head to the front desk and request an item for fingerprinting," Lt. Rozzoro said. Ralph nodded, his sneakers squeaking on the polished floor as he made his exit with an energetic stride that spoke volumes of his excitement.

These junior detectives, she mused, were the future of law enforcement. Training them correctly was imperative, not just for their sake but for the integrity of forensic science and the cases it helped build. It was her duty to ensure they understood the gravity of their responsibilities, the significance of their actions, and the delicate balance they must maintain between solving crimes and preserving individual rights.

As Lt. Rozzoro waited for Ralph's return, she could sense the weight of her role bearing down on her shoulders. The school bus tour was more than just an educational outing; it was a venture into the complexities of human nature and the unwavering quest for truth. In each student's expression, there was a mix of awe and trepidation—a realization that the work they were beginning to understand held the power to change lives irrevocably.

The silent beep of the completed samples interrupted her thoughts, pulling her back into the present. The precision required in these processes always demanded full attention, leaving no room for error. As she prepared the workstation for the next phase, she reiterated silently the same mantra she often drilled into new recruits: *Accuracy above all. Every print can break a case.*

A few moments later, the rhythmic curb of sneakers signaled Ralph's return, his pace hurried and purposeful. As he re-entered the lab, clutching an object tightly in his hand, Lt. Rozzoro felt a renewed determination. This lesson was more than instruction—it was preparation. Preparation for the real world, where the difference between freedom and incarceration could hinge on the minutiae of a single fingerprint line.

The stage was set; the student's journey into the intricate world of forensic fingerprinting had truly begun.

THE FRONT DESK OF THE ST. LOUIS POLICE DEPARTMENT headquarters bustled with the early morning activity as Sgt. Henderson sifted through paperwork, his mind swathed in the lingering haze of a caffeine-deprived night shift. The rhythmic tapping of keyboards filled the air, interspersed with occasional radio chatter.

Just then, a young student burst through the lobby doors, his breaths quick and shallow, eyes wide with a blend of excitement and urgency. "Sgt. Henderson," the boy gasped, clutching at a stitch in his side, "Lt. Rozzoro sent me for something to fingerprint. She said anything unprocessed would work."

Sgt. Henderson blinked, his brow furrowing in confusion. *What was Rozzoro thinking? She knows this is bad business practice.* His protective instincts flared momentarily, his mind racing over the myriad of evidence and personal items cluttered across his desk. Spare keys, a tardy report, a coffee cup stained with forgotten sips—none of which seemed suitable or safe for a classroom demonstration.

"What's your name, kid?" Sgt. Henderson asked, already opening drawers to widen his search.

"Ralph Henry," the boy replied, his voice teeming with both respect and anticipation. He watched Sgt. Henderson closely, drawn by the aura of dedication radiating from the officer, silently wishing to learn from him someday.

Sgt. Henderson grabbed a pair of headphones, their black surface speckled with the fingerprints of hurried use. The handling of this small object held gravity. A trust between officer and student was forged just as fingerprints etched themselves upon the smooth plastic.

"These are Jason Fall's—you know the UPS driver? Make sure you bring them back; they mean something to him." Sgt. Henderson's voice softened, the authority tempered with an underlying concern, showing that he understood the importance of guidance and responsibility.

Ralph nodded earnestly, accepting the headphones as though they were a precious artifact. "I will, sir. Thank you."

He spun on his heel, darting back towards the fingerprint lab. The headphones felt heavier with meaning as he clutched them, a tangible connection to the lives revolving within the police station's orbit. With each step, his heartbeat synchronized with the rhythmic patter of footsteps through the bustling corridors, his thoughts dancing between the eagerness to impress and the fear of disappointment.

Sgt. Henderson watched Ralph disappear down the hallway, a fleeting sense of pride mingling with his habitual vigilance. The boy's zealous approach reminded him of his younger self, full of aspirations and a relentless drive to seek justice. He sighed, turning back to his desk, re-engaging with the endless tide of tasks, yet unable to fully shake the lingering worry about the integrity of every piece of evidence entrusted to him.

As Ralph re-entered the fingerprint lab, clutching the pair of headphones tightly, he couldn't help but feel a surge of exhilaration. The room buzzed with anticipation, all eyes turning towards him with a mix of curiosity and newfound respect. Lt. Rozzoro smiled warmly at him; her gaze acknowledged his swift return.

The space felt charged, needles of adrenaline pricking every corner. It was no longer just a lab; it was a crucible where futures were forged, secrets unearthed, and the bridge between naivety and the adult world was crossed. Ralph stepped into that crucible, headphones held aloft, knowing that these fingerprints carried stories—both mundane and profound.

In the interplay of shadows cast by the overhead fluorescents, the connection between mentor and mentee grew stronger. The fingerprinting lesson continued, yet every brush with evidence seemed now emblazoned with a deeper purpose. The characters danced to an unseen conductor's symphony, every movement laced with an undercurrent of mystery, each touch an echo of trust forged in the crucible of collaboration.

LT. ROZZORO RESUMED HER LESSON, THE UNPROCESSED headphones lying in front of her like a challenge she was eager to meet. The lab softened under the sterile fluorescent light, shadows dancing along the metallic workbenches. She felt the students' eyes on her, wide with curiosity and anticipation, their youthful faces a stark contrast to the severity of the room.

"Alright, everyone, gather around," she instructed, her voice measured yet fervently, reflecting the seriousness of the task at hand. "Today, we're going to collect fingerprints using magnetic powder and collection tape. It may seem straightforward, but every step is critical." She demonstrated the technique with deliberate precision, her movements fluid and controlled. "First, we dust the surface with the magnetic powder. Watch closely; a light touch is all it takes. Too much pressure can smear the ridges, and we lose vital details."

As she explained, her thoughts wandered to the gravity of her role. The room carried the weight of numerous unsolved cases, each piece of evidence a silent witness to a myriad of crimes. In the back of her mind, the ongoing terror unfurled—a city on edge, two predators lurking, and the innocent standing accused. The memory of Mason Mind abandoned at a scene he couldn't recall stirred an uneasy amalgam of pity and dread.

She glanced at the students, who were mesmerized, their excitement almost tangible. These eager faces didn't yet grasp the burden their future professions held. "Once you've applied the powder, use the collection tape to lift the fingerprints. Ensure it's smooth, with no bubbles or wrinkles. Precision, as you'll learn, is non-negotiable." Her tone, firm yet nurturing, was a reflection of her dual role as educator and protector of justice.

As the fingerprints materialized, she felt a flicker of pride in their intrinsic beauty—unique patterns that told the stories of hidden lives, often marred by violence or deceit. This artistry required not just skill but an ethical compass. "We're after three sets of prints today. Remember, each print can be a piece of the puzzle, bringing us closer to the truth or misleading us entirely if handled carelessly."

Her thoughts swirled back to the overarching case. Precision wasn't just a buzzword—it was the lifeline between solving a mystery and letting another body fall amidst the storm. Especially now, with Hear No Evil and the Torrential Terror turning the city into their grisly playground, the stakes were unforgivingly high. The notion of mistaken identity or an overlooked clue gnawed at her, weaving anxiety into her meticulous routine.

She continued, "Look closely. Here we have one print. Identify the points where ridges diverge or form loops—these are called minutiae, and they're crucial in matching fingerprints. We can ascertain a person's identity through these distinct patterns. Without these finer details, our efforts could be futile." Her hands moved with inherent expertise over the headphones, lifting two more sets of prints.

Once the prints were collected, they entered the data into the lab's mainframe, a digital fortress of cross-referenced identities and histories. Each fingerprint was scanned into the computer system, awaiting its fate— a small but significant contest between the past's silent testimony and the relentless pursuit of justice.

As the fingerprints transferred into the database, Lt. Rozzoro thought about the fine line between heroism and fallacy, the needed accuracy of fingerprints. She hoped the students appreciated not just the science but the moral responsibility intertwined with their duties. It wasn't merely about capturing lines and swirls; it was about holding a lifeline to truth, and sometimes, redemption.

While the computer processed, the silence around them felt heavy, mirroring the tension rippling through the department. Every beep and flicker from the monitors underscored the lab's critical role in an ongoing narrative, where success wasn't just rewarded but demanded.

The fingerprints were now in the database, moments away from delivering revelations. Lt. Rozzoro watched the screen with the kind of vigilance born from years of understanding the fragility of evidence. This lesson to the students carried more than forensic knowledge—it imparted the profound significance of their actions and how careful scrutiny in these quiet corridors could reverberate throughout the city's restless nights.

As she awaited the results, Lt. Rozzoro's chest tightened with the unspoken fears of every detective. She had imparted wisdom today, but what awaited them in the light of day still lay hidden, cloaked in suspense and uncertainty. Rozzoro's thoughts were interrupted by an enthusiastic student, "Lt. Rozzoro, seeing that we know where the evidence came from, is it protocol to rule out the fingerprints we know are on it.

THE SHRILL SOUND OF THE COMPUTER ALARM SHATTERED THE focused silence of the fingerprint lab, causing the young students to jolt in their seats. Their faces, lit by the pale glow of the monitors, turned towards Lt. Rozzoro with curiosity and anticipation. An air of seriousness enveloped the room as the Lieutenant moved towards the blinking screen, her demeanor calm but her mind racing. Lt. Rozzoro head tilted to the side as a smile slide on her face, "Awesome question Laurence, and you are absolutely right."

She squinted slightly at the monitor, her fingers dancing over the keyboard as she navigated the database results. The first set of prints, predictably, belonged to Sgt. Henderson. She exhaled softly, documenting the find with practiced ease; the only sound in the room now was the tapping of keys and the faint hum of the computer systems. But then, her eyes lingered on the second match. Ralph Henry. Her heartbeat quickened —a student here, part of today's group. Questions surged in her mind. Why was his fingerprint in the database? We ran their fingerprints six weeks ago and found nothing.

She turned towards Ralph, who stood uncertainly beside his class-mates, his youthful face a picture of confusion and innocence. "Ralph, can you step into the hallway with me for a moment?" she asked, her voice steady but edged with a heaviness that only those entrenched in law enforcement could understand.

Ralph's eyes widened, but he nodded, shuffling behind Lt. Rozzoro as she led him out of the bustling lab into the quieter corridor. Away from the curious eyes of his peers, she felt a wave of anxiety mingling with her sense of duty. The corridor offered a stark contrast to the warm, educational aura of the lab—its sterile white walls felt claustrophobic.

"I need to ask you something," she began, her tone professional but gentle. "Your fingerprints matched records in the database. Can you explain why?"

Ralph blinked, his forehead creasing with worry. "The database? But I've never... Oh, wait. I think it might be because of the Boy Scouts. We did a fingerprinting activity for a merit badge last month," he explained. Relief colored his words, but uncertainty still clouded his expression.

The database operated as a linchpin in modern policing—a tool so invaluable it might as well have been a second heartbeat for the department. Consolidating fingerprints from countless jurisdictions accelerated the identification of suspects, effectively tilting the scale in favor of justice, no matter how elusive it was. As Lt. Rozzoro stood in that dimly lit hallway, the weight of its responsibility pressed upon her. This database was a double-edged sword—its efficiency was unmatched, yet it demanded precision and careful scrutiny of every piece of data, lest an innocent be wrongfully implicated.

She let out a breath she didn't realize she was holding. "Alright, Ralph. It seems like that's a likely explanation. Just needed to make sure." She offered him a reassuring smile, though her mind was already drifting back to the rapid implications and possible pitfalls of their ever-growing reliance on advanced forensic technology.

As they walked back to the lab, an unspoken connection formed between them—lieutenant and student—each learning a different yet crucial lesson about the depth and breadth of justice and technology's role in navigating it.

Guiding him back to the lab, the coldness of the hallway gave way to a sudden warmth between the two. It was an unspoken understanding, a moment of shared humanity amidst the chilling backdrop of their professional roles. The respect she felt for Ralph grew, rooted in his straightforward honesty. She hoped the boy understood the gravity of the environment he was within and how easily perceptions could twist in the shadows.

Inside the lab, the sterile smell of cleaning agents was a stark reminder of the world they inhabited—a world riddled with vile realities and twisted minds. The other students awaited them in a bubble of tension. Students eyed Ralph with a mix of concern and curiosity. Lt. Rozzoro raised a hand, signaling them to settle down. "We're all good," she announced calmly, "just a minor misunderstanding. Let's get back to our lesson."

The computer screen still glowed, its digital display incongruous against the backdrop of human emotions swirling within the room. As they stepped back in, a red alert blinked persistently on the monitor; it flashed an ominous signal that pulled Lt. Rozzoro back into the present turmoil.

Moments of reprieve were fleeting in their line of work, she mused. The real dangers—the serial killers lurking in the city—remained a stark reminder that fear and paranoia were constants. The room quieted, the hum of the computer serving as an uneasy soundtrack to their thoughts.

Lt. Rozzoro's eyes locked onto the screen, the red alert pulling them all back into the harsh reality of their situation. For a brief instant, she looked at Ralph, their shared glance cementing the bond formed in those tense moments of questioning. He may have been innocent in this, but the world they were part of didn't afford them the luxury of ignorance.

Despite the emotional whirlwind, Lt. Rozzoro knew that the next step would only plunge her deeper into the complex web they were all entangled in. Everyone in this room was a piece on a deadly chessboard, their moves dictated by an unseen game master. Fingerprints, merit badges, and the naive excitement of youth were all underpinned by a city gripped in fear.

She approached the computer, her professional demeanor sliding back into place. There were always more clues, more threads leading to the tangled mess. The red alert wasn't just a signal; it was a siren call to the ongoing dangers they had to face, a chilling reminder that the true battle was far from over.

Yet before she could completely shift her focus back to the training, the computer screen began to blink. A new alert—red and insistent—cut through the room's returning peace. Her eyes locked onto the screen, trying to understand the urgency this new message carried. The fingerprints they were examining connected to an ongoing case, a stark reminder of how close shadows of past crimes could come to their current, seemingly benign acts of learning.

Lt. Rozzoro's stomach tightened. She stole a glance at the faces around her—innocent, eager, oblivious to the darker threads weaving through their seemingly mundane activities. Gathering herself, she prepared to unravel yet another layer of their investigation; her resolve hardened with every beat of her heart. Another chapter in the ongoing battle for justice portended ahead, waiting to be written.

LIEUTENANT LISA ROZZORO'S FINGERS TREMBLED AS SHE HELD the phone, a cold dread seeping into her bones. The fingerprint lab's sterile, fluorescent lighting buzzed insistently overhead, casting harsh angles on the clean, white countertops. She dialed the number to the front desk, her other hand gripping the edge of the counter as if to steady herself against an invisible weight.

"Sergeant Henderson, it's Lisa," she said, her voice tight with mounting anxiety.

"Yes, Lieutenant?" Sgt. Henderson spoke with his familiar, steady tone from the other end.

Lisa took a deep breath, mindful of the student's presence in the lab. She turned her back slightly to shield her conversation. "I need to know who owns the headphones the student brought in for fingerprinting."

There was a pause before Sgt. Henderson replied. "Those belong to Jason, the UPS delivery guy."

A sickening lurch twisted Lt. Rozzoro's stomach. "Are you sure, Sergeant?"

"Positive, he left them here the other day. What's this about?" Sgt. Henderson's tone wavered, a crack in his usual demeanor.

Lt. Rozzoro felt a tightening in her throat. Clearing her voice, she explained, "The fingerprints on the headphones match those from the box with the severed head inside." Which prompted Sgt. Henderson's response, "Well, his fingerprints would be on the box. He delivered it."

"I know that, Sergeant," she instantly replied sarcastically. "But it also matched a partial fingerprint from the inside of the box."

A heavy silence laden with the gravity of the revelation filled the air. Lt. Rozzoro could almost feel the tension on the other end of the line. Sgt. Henderson's exhale was audible—a long, labored sound that conveyed more than words ever could.

"No," he finally whispered, disbelief dancing with betrayal. "It can't be."

The phone barely clung to its cradle, Sgt. Henderson's grip slacked as memories of Jason flooded his mind. They had known each other for years, their friendship forged in the crucible of shared experiences, both personal and professional. Jason had been his rock during his wife's last bout with cancer, and Sgt. Henderson had stood by Jason during his divorce. The two had swapped countless stories over late-night beers, their laughter echoing past heartaches and triumphs in equal measure.

Sgt. Henderson's thoughts spiraled into a flashback: a humid summer night, the two sitting on Jason's parent's porch, sipping beer and sharing tales of their youth. Jason's laugh had been infectious, lighting up even the darkest corners of their shared struggles. It seemed impossible to reconcile that image with the possibility lurking in Lt. Rozzoro's revelation.

"Lieutenant?" Sgt. Henderson's voice was a strained murmur. "We can't jump to conclusions."

"Believe me, I don't want to," Lt. Rozzoro replied, her tone a mix of sorrow and urgency. "But the fingerprint is compelling."

A torrent of emotions surged within Sgt. Henderson. The shock of betrayal felt like a physical wound. Could someone he trusted implicitly be capable of such an atrocity? The weight of his badge seemed heavier than ever, his loyalty to Jason warring with his duty as a law enforcement officer.

Back in the fingerprint lab, Lt. Rozzorro couldn't help but feel the echo of Sgt. Henderson's inner turmoil. She knew the evidence pointed in a bleak direction, but she also knew that Jason had been more than a delivery guy to Sgt. Henderson. He had integrated into the fabric of the department because he was always cheerful and reliable. He was the guy everyone turned to for a hand or a joke to lighten the mood.

"Had they all been deceived by a careful facade?" Was the question that gnawed at her insides as she looked at the screen, the incriminating fingerprints glowing back at her like an accusation.

Lt. Rozzoro heard Sgt. Henderson's shaky intake of breath before he spoke again, steadier this time. "I need some time to process this, Lieutenant."

"We'll proceed carefully," she assured him, though her heart pounded with foreboding.

Sgt. Henderson put the phone down gently, the action contrasting the storm gathering within him. Images of past camaraderie clashed violently with Lt. Rozzoro's stark revelation. Slowly, he sank into his chair, trying to reconcile the Jason he knew with the monster these new facts suggested.

As Lt. Rozzoro hung up, the weight of the discovery settled around her like an oppressive fog. The clamor of her students' lighthearted chatter seemed a world away, starkly juxtaposed with the grim reality she now faced. She knew there was no time for delay; with a deep breath, she steeled herself for the steps ahead, the faces of past victims haunting the periphery of her thoughts.

Her movements were precise and deliberate as she documented the latest findings. The severed head, a grisly reminder of their failure to catch the killer sooner, forewarned in her mind. The gravity of this new evidence linking Jason couldn't be overstated. She would have to navigate the murky waters of this investigation with the utmost care, always balancing on the knife edge of hope and despair.

Stepping out of the lab, Lt. Rozzoro spotted the reflection of her pale, resolute visage in a glass pane. She understood too well the journey that lay ahead—a twist into the depths of a hidden, sinister world, masked by ordinary walls and familiar faces. She braced for the truths waiting to be unearthed while accepting that there were no certainties -only shadows and fragments.

CHAPTER
SEVEN
THE FBI ACADEMY

Forty anxious police cadets perched on the rims of their seats within the confines of the classroom, the clinking of a pencil on a desk breaking the oppressive silence. The rumor mill whispers, that the FBI might handpick three outstanding cadets, prickled the otherwise suffocatingly thick and still air. Even the mental thunderclouds that cast darkness over Alan Richardson's thoughts was less oppressive than the air in the room.

The identical 98% scores pushed three cadets standing on the precipice of excellence: Selena Rodriguez, Bradley Warren Jr., and Alan himself. Each of the three wrestled with emotions spurred by the recognition of their achievement; yet, it was only Alan's whose roared with the echoes of a father who valued triumph over verging on victory.

Alan's determination was palpable, as solid as the muscle honed from years as a Navy SEAL. The weight of family expectations crushed down on him, carving furrows in his psyche that not even the most grueling training could erase. His father's voice, stern and unyielding, relentlessly pushed him toward perfection. Mental echoes of his father's snarling adage, "Second place is just the first loser," hammered in Alan's brain and rhythmic alignment with every beat of his heart.

Today was the final exam. A behemoth of tests was a make-or-break challenge whose results would map out the future paths of all cadets. Alan envisioned a future path that progressed from his experience as a Navy SEAL and led to the doorway to the FBI, but knew he had to go through the police department first. The repetition of his father's adage, questions about his future, and his concentration within the moment functioned as metaphorical hawks circling their prey. Although today's stakes were no higher than usual, they felt colossal, even more intimidating than facing death.

Perspiration beaded on Alan's forehead, his gaze fixated more on the glacially moving clock than the questions in front of him. Time was both the enemy and the taskmaster. The repetitive tick-tock was a metronome of escalating dread.

All around him, cadets scribbled furiously, pencils moving with rhythmic certainty. Minor exchanges between them only heightened the tension. "Did you get to the jurisdictional law section?" a cadet whispered. "Yeah, but I skipped it to come back later," another whispered back.

Flashes of memory bombarded Alan—nights spent under the weight of his fatigues, sand, and grime clinging to every pore as he trained in the harshest environments. Every failure, every stumble in training, came crashing back. But those failures had sculpted him into relentless precision. Mistakes were zealously cataloged as lessons never to be repeated.

Yet today, here in this stifling room, those lessons felt distant. Alan's mind replayed moments from his childhood: his father's relentless drilling and preaching an ideology where excellence was the only option. "You can be the best, Alan," his father's voice rasped through time, "but you can't be anything if you're second."

The exam continued, question after torturous question. Alan knew he was prepared. Every sleepless night, every early morning jog through the fog-shrouded streets reinforced by his burdensome borderline insomnia— all of it should have readied him. And yet, the flickering images of his upbringing—the competitions, the accolades, and the disappointment of missed marks—strummed through him like a dissonant chord.

Alan could sense the waning time creeping over his shoulder. In his gut, a knot tightened until it could twist no further. Everything - his future and the goals he had worked towards - appeared nebulous and shifting.

Alan's day always began in a haze of exhaustion, as though a film of grit coated his mind. He would rise before dawn, his body buzzing with an anxious energy that had become both a curse and a perverse blessing. The academy stood imposing every morning, a fortress of expectations that he had to conquer. Classes at the police academy were rigorous, filled with information dense enough to occupy every waking thought and bled into his few hours of sleep.

Workouts were his salvation, physical exertion a way to drown out the noise in his head. Each rep and set were a fight against himself as sweat poured and his muscles burned. He would return to his cramped apartment, dinner spread across cluttered surfaces, textbooks open to chapters he pretended to digest while his mind wandered. Two hours, maybe three, of fitful sleep followed, marked by tossed sheets and muttered dreams.

At midnight, when the world around him seemed submerged in silvery silence, Alan slipped out of his apartment away from gnawing insomnia. He would walk, not to escape his restlessness but to face it head-on. The neighborhood transformed under the ghostly glow of streetlights, an eerie stillness that both comforted and unsettled him. Ghosts of memories flitted through the shadows—his time with the Navy SEALs, nights spent under a foreign sky, eyes scanning the horizon for danger.

Tonight, a rare cool breeze cut through the usual onerous air. Alan stuffed his hands into his jacket pockets, his breath misting faintly. The nightly pilgrimage through streets he knew intimately served as both anchor and release. It sharpened his instincts as a detective and honed his senses to the whispers of the night. Despite the solitude, he felt an odd camaraderie with those who roamed these hours—other insomniacs, graveyard shift workers, and the specters of unresolved cases that never granted peace.

Most of his nocturnal sojourns included revisiting his father's words. But tonight, the forthcoming FBI recruitment clouded his mind and cast long shadows over his steps. The pressure was tangible and crushing as he replayed every mistake and every misstep.

A familiar rumble broke through his reverie. A police cruiser drifted by, headlights cutting swathes of light through the darkness. The driver's window slid down a couple of inches, and Officer Nash gave a knowing nod. "Nightwalker," he murmured in acknowledgment.

Alan lifted a hand in greeting, a small smile touching his lips. Nash and the others who patrolled these late hours knew him well. There was an unspoken bond between those who hunted the night, a shared understanding of sleepless hours and relentless determination. The honks and brief comments from the night-shift officers were a tapestry of camaraderie woven into his walks.

He passed a closed diner, its neon sign flickering out another broken call of ambiance. The smell of stale grease and coffee ghosts lingered. Alan took in the row of forgotten cars along the curb and the distant wail of a siren. Each sound and every scent was a thread in the tapestry of his nocturnal world. A world that felt more real to him than the sunlit one.

Alan's thoughts flitted to the Torrential Terror and Hear No Evil, their dark shadows entwined with his own fears. The weight of the unresolved cases pressed on him, like a vise tightening around his skull. The serial killings weren't just a mystery to be solved but a personal hunt. He needed answers, needed the sense of justice to wake the community from the nightmare that pervaded every rainstorm and every whisper of the wind.

It was nearing three o'clock when he turned back towards home. Early morning dew had begun to form, coating the grass and cement like a cold, clammy blanket. The neighborhood slowly shifted from the realm of echoing silence to the cusp of waking. He quickened his pace, breaking into a light jog, his mind already mapping the day ahead. Another grueling session at the academy, more hours lost in a dance of pretended alertness.

He slid back into his apartment as dawn's fingers stretched across the sky, the small space greeting him like a sanctuary and a prison simultaneously. Stripping off his jacket, Alan ran a hand through his hair, leaving a trail of tension in its wake. He knew there would be no rest, only another march to the academy, chasing an elusive peace of mind and momentary respite from his unyielding commitment. The stakes were too high to allow even a moment's falter. With weary determination, Alan prepared once more to face the quiet chaos of his world.

To Alan, the room was constricting, like a tightening noose. He sat at his school desk, his foot tapping an erratic staccato against the floor tiles, his eyes darting between the clock on the wall and the question paper in front of him. A bead of sweat trickled down his temple, the air tasted of stale coffee and the sharp tang of antiseptics. The final exam was in its last stages, and every tick of the clock gnawed at his nerves.

Alan's hand, clammy and tense, gripped his pencil so tightly that his knuckles began to whiten. His breath came in shallow gasps as he stared down at the last question—the city controller question. The one he had seen before, but now, when it mattered most, the explanation eluded him like a wisp of smoke. His father's voice pierced his concentration. "First place or failure," repeated in a baritone growl that demanded perfection while scoffing at second place.

Alan blinked hard, trying to recall the answer was like trying to catch a fish with his bare hands—slippery, elusive. His heart thudded in his chest, a drumbeat of enduring doom. The stern-faced proctor, Ms. Ann, began to move down the aisles, the clicking of her heels punctuating the heavy silence. Alan's eyes shot to the clock again—two minutes left. A sense of paralysis had gripped his senses, a stark counter to the usual clarity that helped him through Navy SEAL missions and training drills.

The memory of his last test failure clawed its way to the surface—a chemistry exam in high school where he had blanked out. His father's disappointment, a silent but palpable presence in their home afterward, had been a rancid wound that festered for weeks. Every failure piled up against him, a weight pressing on his shoulders, threatening to crush him under its insidious presence.

"Focus, damn it!" Alan muttered under his breath, earning a side glance from Bradley Warren Jr., who was scribbling with the calm assurance that grated on Alan's fraying nerves. Selena Rodriguez, sitting two rows ahead, exuded a calm confidence as she wrote, her pencil moving in an unwavering rhythm. Alan envied her focus, her seeming invulnerability to the mounting pressure that contorted his insides.

Finally, the moment that gnawed hardest arrived. The proctor's eyes swept the room sternly, calling "TIME" with an authority that brooked no argument. Desperate and wild-eyed, Alan hastily filled in answer C - almost certain of its wrongness even as he shaded the circle. The clarity of a missed opportunity washed over him in a cold wave.

"No!" his mind screamed in immediate protest. It was wrong. It had to be wrong. The correct answer was B. He was sure of it now, convinced he had thrown away his chance by giving in to the wrong impulse. The sensation of dread pooled in his stomach, cold and heavy, as the impact of his possible failure sank in.

Throwing his pencil down, Alan stormed out of the classroom, shoving his chair back with a violent motion. The door's handle felt cool and unwelcoming in his grip as he swung it open and stepped into the hallway. The mistakes of past exams, his father's rigid expectations, and the weight of this singular moment—all converged into a suffocating darkness that he struggled to navigate.

The classroom's door swung shut behind him, a solitary sobering sound against the murmur of speculation left behind. This single moment was the difference between everything and nothing. The breadth and depth of the stakes presented in this moment seemed more imposing than Alan had anticipated. He could almost hear his father's disappointed sigh in the silence, the long shadow of expectation cast even within these hallowed halls. The lamp of certainty flickered, struggling to steadfastly flame against the tempests of self-doubt.

Inside the classroom, the other cadets exchanged glances, tension palpable in the air. Some shook their heads, whispering among themselves. Bradley raised an eyebrow while Selena stole a final look at the clock. Alan's outburst was a reminder that for many, beneath their surface decorum lay a seething pit of anxiety. Each cadet carried their invisible burdens, the shared space amplifying their silent struggles.

Bursting into the restroom, Alan felt a surge of hot, fierce frustration. "Damn it," he muttered, his voice echoing off the tiled walls, a ghostly reminder of the pressure cooker he had just been in. He slapped the faucet handle, letting icy water gush forth. Cupping his hands, he splashed his face repeatedly, bracing against the cold as if it could freeze the chaotic swirl of his thoughts. The reflection staring back at him from the mirror was both familiar and alien—a man who should be composed, given his Navy SEAL training, yet visibly fraying at the edges. Alan rubbed his temples, trying to push away the image of his father's steely eyes. He remembered his father's distant look when he had brought home a report card with less-than-perfect grades, the lines of disappointment etched deeper than spoken words could convey. When Alan looked again at the mirror, his reflection bore the indelible stamps of inadequacy and self-doubt.

Alan paced the restroom, muttering obscenities to himself about the exam in a frenzied cadence that matched the turmoil inside his head. He could hear the voices from the past, his father's critiques, each one a dagger twisting whenever he came up short, whenever he did not meet the impossibly high bar set for him. Everything seemed a test. Each failure a mark against him in his father's eyes, straining their already tenuous bond. How could he, a member of the elite Navy SEALs, crumble under the pressure of an exam? How would he face his father?

His father's subtle but crushing expressions of disapproval had made Alan into this ball of taut nerves and apprehension. He desperately wanted to break free, to rise above this suffocating weight that pressed down on him. But his efforts missed their mark. Every minute, failure bound him tighter, intensifying the feeling of being trapped as a legacy of disappointment coiled around his spirit.

As he exited the restroom, each step felt like dragging his feet through a mire of dread. He couldn't shake the gnawing certainty that he had marked the wrong answer, and with it, jeopardized everything he had worked for. The potential failure was a compilation of the father's expectations, his own relentless drive for perfection, and the brutal truth of competition.

THE RESTROOM DOOR SQUEAKED OPEN, BREAKING HIS fraught reverie. Cadet Charles Manning, strolled in, eyes bright and mouth curved into a grin. "Hey, Richardson!" he called. "Congrats on finishing the test. Feels great, doesn't it? We're finally at the end."

Alan forced a tight smile, his insides knotting further at the cadet's nonchalance. "Yeah, something like that," he replied in a voice that contradicted his inner turmoil of envy and frustration. How do they do it? Alan questioned himself, jealousy licking at his insides, seeing others bask in the certainty of their success.

Gnawing on his lip, Alan's mind clung desperately to the city controller's question. He turned abruptly to Manning. "Manning, how'd you answer the city controller question?" His voice carried the edge of urgency, almost pleading. "*89. The city controller does not agree to the search and the basis that he is an elected official. Which of the following states his position in another way?*"

Manning paused, his brow furrowing as he recalled. "Oh, that one? It was B. Community budget oversight. We covered it last month, remember?"

The admission hit Alan like a thunderclap. His shoulders slumped, his head dropping forward in sheer disgust. The tension inside him snapped; he had known it, lodged somewhere in the recesses of his mind. "I knew it," he muttered, the words tasting bitter on his tongue. He blinked rapidly, resisting the tidal wave of humiliation rising within him.

Alan exhaled a defeated sigh. Then he turned on his heel and trudged toward the door, burdened with his perceived shortcomings and teetering on the edge of despair. The relentless pursuit of perfection pulled him into an abyss he feared he could not climb out of. The weight of the upcoming results, coupled with the incessant pressure of his role as a police officer, settled like a stone in his chest.

He exited the restroom, the murmur of the cadets rising in a dull roar around him. As he merged back into the flow of students, his mind was elsewhere, grappling with the shadows of inadequacy and the oppressive fear of what his future might now hold.

ALAN RICHARDSON LUNGED DOWN THE CORRIDORS OF THE academy, a tempest brewing inside. His heart pounded in rhythm with his hurried footsteps, a dire symphony of pulses echoing the stakes that weighed upon him. He could hear the murmurs of his peers—distant yet close, like whispers cascading into his frenzied mind. The test results were out. Frantic energy spurred him.

As he entered the classroom, a wave of tension hit him. Dozens of cadets' faces, etched with nervous anticipation, crowded around Ms. Ann, the proctor. Her resolute presence juxtaposed the frenzy of expectation threading through the room. Alan's eyes scanned the space for Cadets Selena Rodriguez and Bradley Warren Jr., the two names now synonymous with competition and pressure. Selena's calm poise, standing apart from the crowd, exuded an effortless confidence. Bradley, on the other hand, flickered with a contained restlessness that mirrored Alan's own.

Ms. Ann's crisp voice sliced through the quiet chaos: "Congratulations, cadets. Your hard work has not gone unnoticed. I have the final exam results here." Her formality felt all too sterile against the cadets' palpable anxiety.

One by one, the cadets' fates were revealed with the announcement of their scores. Alan clenched his fists, knuckles whitening as Ms. Ann's gaze finally landed on them—the top three. Her eyes held a knowing glint, a sliver of the power she held in those next few spoken words.

"Selena Rodriguez," Ms. Ann announced, "ninety-seven percent—first place."

A scattered applause drifted through the classroom, but Alan barely registered it. His focus was fractured between the now and the what-if. Selena's impassive smile, a simple curve that conveyed untouchable success, gnawed at the edge of his resolve. He remembered the hours they had sparred over case studies. She always seemed a step ahead. Now wasn't any different. But nothing felt the same.

Ms. Ann continued, "We have a tie for second place..." Alan held his breath. Time stretched thin, seconds dragging as his pulse sped up. Each beat resonated with primal urgency.

"Alan Richardson and Bradley Warren Jr. both scored ninety-six percent," she said, her tone unwavering.

The words crashed onto him with the weight of inevitability and despair. Alan's gaze darted to Bradley, whose broad frame seemed to shrink under the revelation. The tension between them was a silent duel over dominance and destiny. Alan's mind spiraled—with thoughts about what his score means for FBI recruitment and his father's admonishments about second place.

One thought escaped as Alan shouted across the increasingly hushed room, "What does this tie mean for FBI recruitment?"

Ms. Ann's face remained calm, though the room crackled with the unsaid implications. "Both of you will be considered," she replied, her voice taut with inflexible neutrality, "but the final decision remains with the recruitment board."

Alan's stomach churned as her answer left a cavernous uncertainty. His vision blurred slightly, the room's stark lines and figures smudging into a fog. The proctor's controlled composure felt like a cold shutter against his rising panic.

Bradley's eyes locked onto Alan's for a moment, a fierce blend of rivalry and reluctant camaraderie. In that shared glance, history flickered—

a series of competitions, late-night strategy sessions, and mutual encouragement transformed by pressure into rivalry. The academy had fostered their ambitions and driven a wedge between their shared potential.

Selena's contentment simmered in the background, a constant reminder of the perfection he could not quite grasp. Her previous victories, small but consistent, dug into his insecurities. She carried the aura of someone born for greatness, her path unimpeded by gnawing internal doubt.

Alan's presence was a cold bubble amidst the numerous conversations buzzing around him. His shoulders slumped involuntarily, a rare lapse in his otherwise stiff presence. He could feel the stares of the other cadets gauging his reaction and weighing his strength. But inside, he was already questioning every step taken to this moment—a battlefield of lingering self-doubt cloaked in the regimented cadence of his past.

The proctor's voice continued in the background, a thread of order against the rising conversations. Alan barely registered the final announcements, cadet names blending into a muddled mess of insignificant details. He was fixated on the second-place tie, its meaning, and how it could unravel all his work.

He exited the room, seeking clarity and striving to navigate the growing uncertainty lodging itself in his path. Alan knew a momentary lapse now could shatter his future, but his steps could not chase away the specter of doubt tightly gripping him.

CHAPTER
EIGHT
THE NIGHTWALKER

Alan sat in his office, a dimly lit sanctuary buried within the labyrinthine police department. The ambient hum of computers and the monotonous murmur of his colleagues provided a backdrop he had almost grown accustomed to. Paper scraps littered his desk in chaotic disarray. Each scrap was filled with notes and theories—silent testaments to the grim dance of death being played out in the city.

He took a deep breath, rubbing his temple as his mind traveled to the morbid characters that occupied his thoughts. "The Enucleator," the nightmarish figure who removed eyes as though performing some dark ritual of control, haunted his every waking moment. His actions were methodical, almost surgical—a perverse form of artistry that Alan found both repulsive and fascinating. Then there was "The Torrential Terror." These brutal killings were masked by the chaotic ferocity of violent rainstorms. The profoundly unsettling imagery of bodies found soaked, each a victim of a killer who seemed to thrive in pandemonium, using the elements as an accomplice.

Alan's chair creaked as he leaned back, brooding over the disquieting possibility that gnawed at his mind. Were there truly two predators prowling the city, or was there just one, an individual with a fragmented psyche, skilled in the art of deception? Perhaps they were twin personas, each with their own distinct signature, united in a grotesque ballet of destruction. The thoughts of who or what he might be hunting were enough to make his pulse quicken. *Are these two the same serial killer? Why would Stacy Rhymes, the reporter gives the same killer two names? I guess reporters will do anything to sell papers!*

Flashes of headlines and news broadcasts flittered through his mind. The media had seized these ghastly monikers, reveling in the sensation they generated. "The Enucleator" and "The Torrential Terror"—names that rolled off the tongue with twisted elegance, feeding a morbid curiosity. Alan felt a wave of frustration wash over him. The public, enraptured by these theatrical nicknames, seemed detached from the gruesome reality, more enamored with the horror story than the victims who lay in its wake. This was no sideshow but a real and terrifying distortion of life, each act of violence a stark reminder of humanity's fragile grip on normalcy.

His eyes fell upon a photograph pinned up on his wall—a stark, candid capture of one of the crime scenes. He couldn't help but feel the urgency tighten around him. Time was a relentless tide that showed no mercy for the lives at stake. He squinted at the picture as if it held some unspoken clue that had yet to reveal itself. A gnawing thought twisted inside him. He needed clarity, a fresh perspective, and maybe even a bit of luck.

And then his thoughts converged on Stacy Rhymes. The reporter was something of an anomaly herself—doggedly persistent, unafraid to tread where others dared not go. She had a knack for finding the hidden threads within the labyrinth of the media's sensationalist web. Perhaps she had uncovered something—some nuance missed by the detectives and the analysts who poured over the data. Maybe she had some information that could pierce the shroud of uncertainty enveloping the case.

Alan felt a flicker of determination within him, small but undeniably present. This was the path forward. He would reach out to Stacy, dive into her wells of knowledge, and extract any insight that could cast light upon these malevolent forces at play. In the swirling mists of his contemplation, the resolve took root—he needed to contact her quickly. Urgency whispered in his ear, pushing him into action against the encompassing shadows of doubt.

With newfound purpose, Alan swept the scattered papers into a semblance of order and rose from his chair. The weight of the unsolved cases pressed against his shoulders, but a spark of hope carried him out of the office and into the blurring frontier between darkness and revelation.

ALAN STOOD IN THE DIM OFFICE LIGHT, THE SOFT BUZZ OF THE fluorescent bulbs barely registering through the haze of his thoughts. He collected his belongings in a mechanical fashion—a pen here, a file there—but his mind traveled backward. The reporter's nickname for him—"The Nightwalker"—echoed in the recesses of his memory, pulling him to a time when the title was but a nascent whisper.

That crisp November night, he had woken abruptly, submerged in a sea of thoughts. The darkness outside mirrored his mind, vast and impenetrable. His loft apartment, usually a sanctuary, felt as if it were closing in on him. The newscasts, the case files strewn about, and the photographs of victims were all fragments of a puzzle that seemed to twist further out of reach with each passing day. Without hesitation, Alan decided he needed to clear his head. The moon hung low, casting silver beams that traced the outline of his Navy bootcamp jogging suit as he changed gear. He strapped on his badge, nestled his weapon securely, and tugged his skullcap over his ears. Then, without a glance back, he slipped through the door and into the cool night air.

The city seemed to sleep, blissfully unaware of the storm that raged within Alan's mind. His feet pounded the pavement in a rhythmic cadence, each step an attempt to outpace the clutter of his brain. Moving through the deserted streets of downtown, he noticed the quiet—no traffic, no hum of the city's daily chaos. It was as if the world was holding its breath, which matched the tension in his chest. The sound of his footfalls on asphalt was the only thing grounding him in reality.

He ran towards the Riverfront, the draw of the open space irresistible. The Gateway Arch, with its grand iron curves, stood sentinel against the sky, silhouetted in the cold moonlight. As he approached, Alan's breath puffed in cloudy bursts, the air biting at his exposed skin. He felt as if he were chasing shadows, ghostly remnants of cases past and present. The arch steps rose before him, and, without breaking stride, he launched himself up them, feeling the burn in his calves, the protest in his lungs. This was his pursuit—both literal and metaphorical.

Reaching the apex, Alan paused, bending over to catch his breath, the city sprawling beneath him like a glittering map of unsolved mysteries. The skyline stretched before his vision, and his mind began to click through images—crime scene photos, autopsy reports, killer profiles—each one adding to a mosaic that pointed to something larger, more complex than he had anticipated. The frigid air sharpened the errant flashes of insight, alighting upon a puzzle piece he had yet to connect.

He recalled the moment with the reporter, Stacy Rhymes, who had christened him "The Nightwalker." It was not meant as flattery. To the public, it signified a relentless hunter of the night, but to Alan, it was a reminder of the sleepless battles he waged alone. He often wondered if the title was a curse, isolating him from those who might understand, who could help bear the weight of his nightly vigils.

Night walking was not simply an escape; it was a ritual of clarity. Each mile covered peeled-back layers of his psyche, revealing the raw emotions and fears he buried under the facade of control. The quiet streets amplified his introspection, every silent corner another facet of his relentless pursuit of justice. His thoughts flitted back to the images of the victims -every clue, every misstep weighing heavily on his conscience. The last vestiges of humanity in those grainy pictures nag at him, begging for resolution and peace.

He tried to reconcile his double life. His role in the precinct was clear —apprehend, protect, and serve. But when the sun dipped below the horizon, he transformed into something else, something darker. He was driven by shadows. He was compelled to understand the darkness in others, so that he could shine a light for those left in the abyss. The chill from his perch in the Arch had cemented that understanding, the night air burning his lungs with every breath, a trial by cold fire.

Loneliness crept alongside him, a silent companion on nights like these. Relationships had faded into the background, victims of his relentless quest to walk the night until every lost soul had their story completed. Every choice carried the weight of souls past, each interaction tinged with the unspoken question: Would this be the case that finally broke him or the one that saved another life?

Standing at the top of the Arch steps, Alan felt a measure of resolve settle in his chest. He had made a promise to himself—not one of glory but one of duty—to face the relentless nights, the burdens of the title, and the ghosts of his conscience with unwavering resolve. The winding paths of the Riverfront, with its unseen dangers and unspoken histories, would always be part of his battleground—an endless run towards justice, clarity, and perhaps, one day, peace.

The memory faded as he straightened up, eyes scanning the city below, the heartbeat of the urban night now in sync with his own. With renewed purpose, Alan began the descent, the Riverfront beckoning him toward another unknown path that justice demanded he tread, the flashbacks of his origin becoming the compass guiding him forward.

THE HUM OF NOISE AT THE RIVERFRONT WAS A SYMPHONY OF distant sirens, whispers of water against stone, and the occasional honk from an unseen car. Alan's rhythmic footfalls suddenly became a cacophony to his own ears, almost mismatched with the lull of city night. As he neared the graffiti-covered wall, the street art's vibrant chaos starkly contrasted with the monochrome of his thoughts. Thoughts that were abruptly interrupted.

Three vans, like phantoms materializing out of a shadowed haze, glided past him. Their windows were dark, hiding whatever secrets lay concealed within. Their presence was almost surreal, considering this area and this hour. Alan's instincts sharpened. Suspicion curled around his mind like a fist.

With a quickened pace but maintaining a whisper of stealth, he bolted down the stairs, each step a protest against haste. The discarded memories of cigarette butts, forgotten flyers, and remnants of someone else's evening litter the path down the stairs. He kept his eyes locked on the tail lights, watching them snake through the urban labyrinth until they converged near a warehouse marred by years of neglect and a medley of spray-painted graffiti.

From his vantage point, he saw four figures emerge from the vans. The assault rifles that slung across their bodies augmented their silhouettes.

Their thug armor bathed in the eerie glow of ambient streetlights. Alan could barely make out the two women, their forms shackled, shadows of desperation trailing them into the darkened warehouse.

His breath calmed to a measured cadence, though his heart hammered a staccato rhythm within his chest. Unbidden memories of past stakeouts surged, reminding him of the consequences of rash actions. He knew his arsenal tonight—a single firearm with unforgivingly limited rounds—was barely sufficient to take on such armed adversaries. Tactical thinking would be his greatest ally.

As the image of those women seared onto his mind, his resolve crystallized—he could not, would not, let fear or doubt tether him. Moments from his training flickered past his eyes. Nighttime drills, scenarios built from the worst humanity could offer, and the unyielding drive to protect pulsed through his veins. Each recalled frame galvanized his determination, quietly fueling the fire within him.

Sliding silently along the graffiti-streaked walls, Alan circled around the building, each step calculated to avoid the scattered refuse and broken glass that could betray his presence. His senses strained against the oppressive weight of silence and the noise from the distant city, feeling miles away. His anticipation was rising so much that he could taste it.

At the back, the dim light barely penetrated the acrid blackness. Alan's hand itched to unscrew the lone bulb and mute its sickly glow, a tactic he had employed before to cloak himself in shadows. But weighed down by memories of past failures and that gnawing sense of justice, he opted to delay the approach. Each second stretched like a taut line on a ticking bomb, every move underscored by the silent mantra: get in, get them out.

Shrouded in the moody haze of the night, Alan found his vantage point and observed the warehouse's rear entrance. Flickers of movement within indicated that he wasn't alone. His tactical mind outlined the plan, accounting for the limited ammunition, the necessity of stealth, and most importantly, the rescue.

The determination to act, to unveil the warehouse's grim secrets, pressed against the heavy veil of trepidation. The women's faces—haunted, unknown, yet painfully human—propelled him forward, a reluctant hero in the face of impending calamity. The shadows around the warehouse seemed to pulse with foreboding, yet also with a strange clarity. Each breath, each decision, brought Alan closer to the brink, where action mingled perilously with the thrill of purpose—the mission's true call to justice.

Raindrops skittered across the warehouse's corrugated iron roof; the rhythmic pelting matched Alan's heartbeat. As he crouched behind a rusted dumpster, he observed the lone lookout, illuminated by a streetlamp's yellow gleam. The stench of garbage and wet asphalt assaulted his senses, grounding him in the here and now.

Alan's gaze lifted to the lamp above the lookout. Unscrewing one bulb would shroud the lamp in darkness, a trick he'd learned during a particularly harrowing Navy SEAL exercise. He glanced around, the primal stillness of the night wrapping him like a shroud. With careful precision, he unscrewed the bulb, sending the lookout into an oblivious black void.

Moving in the shadows, Alan neared the distracted guard. Every muscle in Alan's body thrummed—coiled with the latent energy of years spent training in martial arts. Calmness washed over him—the kind of calm borne not of peace but of immense discipline and deadly purpose.

"Drop your weapon and lie on the ground," he ordered, his voice a low growl. The lookout turned, startled, his eyes wide with fear. For a breath, there was hope that compliance might come. But fear can be a dangerous motivator.

The lookout kicked fast and desperately. Alan's weapon was knocked from his grip, and pain exploded in his wrist. Instinct took over. An adrenaline-fueled moment of clarity traced a vivid arc in Alan's mind, mapping every possible countermove.

They clashed beneath the flickering streetlamp, a tableau of violence played out in stark chiaroscuro. Alan dove, sidestepped, and parried, each movement a testament to hours spent in relentless, grueling training. The lookout was no amateur, and he fought with the viciousness of the corner. But for Alan, this was familiar territory—a symphony of chaos that he knew all too well.

He blocked a punch, countering with a swift elbow strike to the man's sternum. His thoughts remained cold, calculating and weighing each motion with surgical precision. He remembered a mission in Kabul where he had disarmed an enemy combatant with similar quick strikes, remaining collected under the hiss of gunfire and the chaos of war. He recalled the face of that adversary, etched with a surprised grimace, the same expression now mirrored in the lookout's eyes.

The lookout faltered, gasping for breath, but launched another desperate attack. Alan dodged, grabbed the man's arm, and leveraged his momentum to throw him to the ground. The crunch of gravel beneath the lookout's fall was a satisfying punctuation to the conflict.

Alan quickly subdued him, swift as a striking serpent, pinning him with his knee and binding his wrists with his own bootlaces. The man struggled, but futility dulled his movements. Alan's mind raced as he stripped the struggle from the essence of the moment and returned to tactical pragmatism.

With the lookout immobilized, Alan grabbed the phone from the man's jacket pocket. The dim light from the device's screen cast an eerie glow over the grit and grime of their battleground. Alan's fingers moved with an assured swiftness as he dialed police headquarters.

"This is Cadet Alan Richardson," he said with controlled urgency. "I've subdued a suspect at the warehouse on Riverfront. I need immediate backup."

He could hear the faint affirmation from the dispatcher, the static-laced acknowledgment reassuring but demanding his sustained vigilance. His surroundings came back into focus, the night stretching its tense silence before him.

He ended the call, his breath a steady metronome to the chaotic symphony. Another memory rose, vivid and clear—the first time he had disarmed an aggressor during basic training. The instructor's voice echoed in his head: "Root yourself in the now. Future and past are distractions."

Alan scanned the area, mindful of the darkness and the fragility of their isolation. The scent of rain-soaked earth mingled with the metallic tang of tension. Each inhale brought not just air but a flood of remembered drills, calculated risks, and lives saved and lost. Tonight, he added new memories to the ledger.

Behind him, the lookout lay moaning faintly—one piece in the larger puzzle Alan was desperate to solve. Every sinew in his body remained taut, every nerve alert—he was a hunter on the precipice of the final takedown.

ALAN'S BREATH FOGGED IN THE CHILLY NIGHT AIR AS HE scanned the area, his eyes darting over the dimly lit alleyways and rooftops. The red neon glimmer of the warehouse sign flickered, casting fleeting shadows on the grimy ground. He could feel his heart thrumming with tension and determination. His hand brushed the rough, weathered brick wall as he moved with calculated precision; his senses heightened. A lonely streetlight buzzed overhead, illuminating patches of the empty street.

Alan assessed his surroundings. An ominous red glow bathed the narrow hallway in front of him. His eyes traced the corridor's length, noting the absence of security cameras but remaining alert for unseen dangers. He took a deep breath, inhaling the faint stench of the city, engine oil, and damp concrete. He proceeded with measured steps, his footsteps camouflaged by the noise of distant traffic.

As he approached the glass-topped door at the hallway's end, Alan's gaze fixed on a sign that read, "Open door slowly." The mantra echoed in his mind as a cautionary reminder. Through the glass, he could make out the shapes of three men sitting at a table engrossed in a card game. Their laughter punctuated the thick silence, a stark contrast to the tension gnawing at Alan's nerves. Yet the girls—the prime reason for his intrusion —remained unseen.

Moments stretched interminably as Alan stood poised by the door, contemplating his next move. The piercing wail of police sirens in the distance sliced through his thoughts, the urgency of their approach accelerating his decision-making. His grip tightened around his weapon as he shouldered the door open.

Alan moved swiftly, his heart pounding louder than ever. In one fluid motion, he raised his firearm and fired a round into the air. The deafening crack echoed off the warehouse walls, startling the men at the table. His voice boomed with the authority born from years of service: "On the ground, now!"

Panic flashed across their faces, replaced by the primal reaction to the immediate threat. Overturned tables, scattered cards, and clattering chairs were all by-products of the men dropping to the floor and lacing their hands behind their heads. The distinct sound of reinforcements arriving grew louder, and Alan knew his timing had been impeccable.

His eyes remained sharp, darting between the suspects and the surroundings, awaiting the arrival of the STLPD. The door burst open, and a flood of officers swept into the room, their movements choreographed by years of practice and mutual trust. Their barked commands echoed Alan's previous orders. The synchronization between Alan and the STLPD spoke of a shared history—a camaraderie forged in the crucible of past operations. Each member knew their part without needing explicit direction.

Alan and the officers moved swiftly to secure the scene. The smells of sweat and fear filled the cold air as Alan and the team leaders worked to subdue and apprehend the suspects. Every hand signal and glance articulated more than words ever could—an implicit language honed through countless high-pressure encounters.

Briefly, while standing in the eye of the operation, Alan allowed himself to feel the intensity of what they were accomplishing. The police action around him was the harmony of justice in action. The trust and cooperation among them underscored their shared commitment to protect the vulnerable and ensure no criminal escaped unpunished.

Within moments, the scene transitioned from chaos to control, and the suspects were cuffed and read their rights. Alan's immediate focus shifted from the apprehended men to the more pressing concern—the missing girls. Even as they recited procedures, his mind raced with images of possible hiding places within the warehouse's sprawling, clandestine corridors.

Tension still hung in the air like an unspent charge. While the impact of what they had just stumbled upon was yet to fully settle, the relief was tempered by the grim anticipation of the lies within the warehouse's depths. Alan's eyes met those of his fellow officers, a silent pledge to uncover and rescue, sparing no effort as they pressed forward into the unknown recesses of the building.

The pulsating wails of distant sirens began to ebb, merging with the night's quiet hum. Alan pressed on, his resolve hardening with every step toward the warehouse's heart, where the truth awaited, cloaked and silent.

THE HOLLOW ECHOES OF FOOTSTEPS REVERBERATED THROUGH the warehouse as Alan stood near the entrance, his fingers still tingling from the adrenaline rush of the confrontation. The lieutenant's stern voice broke the silence, a serrated edge cutting through the air, demanding answers. "What the hell were you thinking, Alan? Going in alone like that? You could've gotten yourself killed!"

Alan steadied his breathing, his mind racing. He rubbed the back of his neck, feeling the grit and sweat mingling there. "I had to act fast," he replied, his voice almost a whisper, barely holding back the tremor of exhaustion. "I couldn't wait for backup, not with those women in danger."

The lieutenant's face was a portrait of controlled fury, his eyes burning with a mix of concern and ire. "Protocol exists for a reason! You taking unnecessary risks just escalates the danger for everyone involved. Not to mention making things more complicated for the entire operation!"

The warehouse's oppressive shadows whispered of hidden atrocities, and the grimy walls were silent witness to countless unspeakable acts. Anger and grief created heat in Alan's chest as he listened. He understood the lieutenant's outrage. Sometimes precious lives hung by a thread too thin and precious to wait for procedures and protocols.

The distant wails of police sirens finally arrived, filling the room with growing intensity. It was not until the sudden, urgent shouts of officers interrupted them that both men turned, their argument forgotten in a moment's flash.

"Lieutenant! Over here!" an officer called out, beckoning them toward a room barely illuminated by the soft afterglow of emergency lights.

As Alan and the Lieutenant followed, they entered a space that was both haunting and heart-wrenching. There were rows of twin-sized beds lining the room. Each was occupied by a handcuffed fear-ridden girl no older than sixteen. Some cried silently, their tears glistening in the limited light; others stared vacantly, trapped between reality and the nightmare that enveloped them.

A stomach-churning realization settled over Alan like a toxic fog. He had interrupted a sex-trafficking operation. The gravity of what he stumbled upon threatened to crush him. His eyes scanned the room, absorbing the horrific scope of the network that thrived hidden in plain sight.

The longer Alan stared, the more the details came into focus. The bruises on the girls' wrists came from where the handcuffs bit into their skin. Their cheeks were gaunt from malnutrition. The lingering scent of fear clung to the air like a ghostly presence. This place was a graveyard of innocence, a stark reminder of the depravity that human beings could inflict upon each other.

Local statistics flashed through his mind. The numbers pointed to a fact he had long tried to ignore: St. Louis had become a burgeoning hub for trafficking due to its central location. Crime networks were operating like a many-headed hydra that law enforcement could not seem to decapitate. For every ring dismantled, a dozen cropped up overnight, fueled by demand and the omnipresent shadow of organized crime.

Jerry, an officer whose presence often lent a calming reassurance, examined a set of file cabinets hurriedly. "Lieutenant," he said, looking up with grim recognition, "we've got records here—names, transactions. This goes deeper than it looks."

Backlit by the grim recognition of the room, the lieutenant turned to Alan, his previous ire now clouded by the profound impact of the discovery. "Do you realize the implications of this?" His voice softened but retained an incredulous edge: "You might have just blown open the largest trafficking ring we've encountered in years."

Caring officers ushered the girls out as Alan watched. Faces, each more haunting than the last, marked his memory. He recognized the immense responsibility placed on his shoulders; one impulsive act had saved them, yet the battle had only just begun.

Feeling the intense pressure of the lieutenant's gaze, Alan finally spoke, more to himself than to anyone else. "They deserve justice. We have to dismantle every single part of this network, no matter the cost."

The lieutenant's features softened marginally, a glimmer of understanding passing between them. "We will," he said with quiet conviction. "But we do it the right way. We can't afford any more risks, Alan. Not you, not the victims. This city needs a meticulous, calculated approach to tackling this monster."

Nodding, Alan felt the weight of the Lieutenant's words. The necessity for solid teamwork and strategic planning was paramount. The stark corridors and dim corners of the warehouse might hold the key to a challenge greater than personal valor. He would need to adhere to procedures while harnessing the raw determination that had driven him here in the first place.

As the scene unfolded, the sorrow and relief intertwined, galvanizing Alan's resolve. He stood there amid the fading echoes of their voices, embracing the cold reality that this was only the beginning. The real work of bringing down the hydra has started now. The stakes had never been higher, but neither had the urgency of their mission.

Reporter Stacy Rhymes ran with the story once it was leaked to the press. From there, Alan Richardson was no longer The Nightwalker. He was now St. Louis's newest nighttime hero, their very own Batman.

CHAPTER
NINE
THE REPORTER

S tacy Rhymes sank into her chair, the leather sighing under the weight of many sleepless nights. The dim light of her early morning office cast long shadows across the cluttered desk, crammed with police reports, autopsy photos, and sketches that told stories of immense horror. The city outside was beginning to wake, the hum of traffic a distant murmur beneath her window, and the first rays of dawn barely pierced the gray clouds, threatening another storm.

She could feel St. Louis's collective anxiety—a city gripped by the recent brutalities of two killers, each inflicting their own brand of ghoulish art. Conversations at coffee shops were hushed. People cast furtive glances outside windows, dreading the next thunderstorm, while parents held their children a little tighter. Fearful anticipation gripped the citizens of St. Louis.

Stacy's fingers danced over her keyboard, her eyes methodically scanning her notes one last time. Her workspace, usually a realm of routine chaos, now felt like the epicenter of something massive and foreboding. She could almost hear the frantic pulse of the city through the drumming of her own heart, each keypress marking the beginning of a new chapter in St. Louis's collective nightmare.

She meticulously outlined the killings, each method more bone-chilling than the last. One killer moved like a phantom within violent rainstorms, leaving behind eyeless victims, their empty sockets a ghastly signature. The other, more calculating and surgical, severed ears with pristine precision, leaving their victims deaf to the whispers of the world. Pinning down these atrocities onto a digital page, Stacy felt the weight of her responsibility to tell their stories with integrity.

She leaned back, her eyes narrowing in contemplation. The names had to strike the right balance. "The Torrential Terror" evoked the almost mythical fear of thunderstorms—elements and eyes ripped asunder in a cruel harmony. It perfectly encapsulated the dread each storm now brought with it. In contrast, "Hear No Evil" carried a sinister simplicity that would chill readers to their cores—a stark reminder of the silence forced upon these victims.

With a final, decisive keystroke, she chose "The Torrential Terror" and confirmed "Hear No Evil." Stacy hovered over the send button, a bead of sweat tracing her temple before dropping to her cheek, her breath steady but shallow. The names would reverberate through every television broadcast, radio show, and conversation over dinner tables. She could already imagine the ripple effect of her words tearing through the city's collective psyche.

Submitting the article to her editor came with a cocktail of anticipation and dread. She watched the editor's eyes flit across the text, his expression shifting from critical analysis to unspoken approval. With his curt nod, the story moved forward, each word paving a path across the city's consciousness.

"Are you sure about this?" asked Alex, a seasoned editor with graying hair and a weary demeanor, leaning against Stacy's desk. "These names... they have weight."

Stacy paused, her blue eyes flickering with a mix of resolve and doubt. "We need names that capture their essence, Alex. Something that sticks, and I think that the Torrential Terror and Hear No Evil are names that will haunt people."

Her words sent a shiver through the nearby reporters who had paused their own tasks to eavesdrop. The names hung in the air, heavy with the promise of fear, and transformed the newsroom into a pressure cooker, ready to burst.

"But 'The Torrential Terror'—do we really want to invoke storms and chaos, make it sound almost mythical?" chimed in Marcy, a younger, ambitious reporter who often challenged Stacy's decisions. Her voice wavered, betraying her own unease. "And 'Hear No Evil,' there's something almost... macabrely poetic about it."

Stacy sighed, running a hand through her blonde hair. "And that's exactly why they work," she retorted, refusing to show any outward crack in her armor. Inside, however, she grappled with the ethical lines she knew she was crossing. "The public needs to wake up and be on alert. These names do that."

Alex frowned, crossing his arms. "But there's a fine line between awareness and exploitation. Think of the victims' families. How will they feel seeing these killers turned into near-legends?"

Her fingers hesitated over the keyboard, a rare moment of stillness. She was a journalist first, but also human. "I get that, Alex. But sensationalism sells papers. And if these names help catch the killers or save lives, isn't it worth it?"

The debate simmered in the room, a pot boiling just shy of spilling over. Tension crackled like static in the air, each colleague's opinion electrifying the atmosphere with conflicting thoughts and feelings. Stacy's internal battle mirrored the storm outside, consisting of thunder and moral quandaries.

Marcy stepped closer, lowering her voice to a near whisper. "Look, I know you care, Stacy, but everyone's going to see those names—kids, parents, survivors. You want them to feel safe, not terrified."

Stacy's eyes met Marcy's, and for a moment, her steely gaze softened. "I want them to be vigilant," she said, her voice gentle but firm. "There's nothing safe about being blissfully unaware of monsters among us."

The newsroom fell silent, the weight of her words sinking deep. Even the phones seemed to pause their incessant ringing in a moment of collective introspection. Finally, Alex nodded, his gruff exterior softening in reluctant agreement.

"Alright," he said, relenting. "The Torrential Terror and Hear No Evil it is—but you better be ready for the backlash."

Stacy offered a small, grim smile. "I always am."

She pivoted back to her screen, the glow reflecting off her determined face as she typed out the final sentences of her article. Each keystroke resonated with purpose, reverberating through the quiet tension of the room. The newsroom resumed its chaotic dance, but the air remained taut, charged with the gravity of their decision.

As the clock ticked closer to noon, Stacy hit 'send' and submitted her article for publication. The finality of the act sent another ripple of silence through the space. She felt the weight of the city's expectations settle on her shoulders, an invisible but palpable burden.

She leaned back in her chair, eyes closed, for a moment to gather her thoughts. The faces of the victims flashed in her mind, their tragic stories fueling her determination. She knew there were no easy answers nor simple resolutions. But in naming the killers, she hoped to shine a light on the shadows that had crept into St. Louis and gripped it with relentless fear.

Moments later, the clicking and clanking of the printing press began to hum through the walls. Stacy walked over to the press room, compelled by the mechanical symphony of progress. Her heart pounded in tandem with the rhythmic beats of the machines, each press and release echoing the importance of the words soon to flood the city.

Moments later, the clicking and clanking of the printing press began to hum through the walls. Stacy walked over to the press room, compelled by the mechanical symphony of progress. Her heart pounded in tandem with the rhythmic beats of the machines, each press and release echoing the importance of the words soon to flood the city.

The first copies emerged, hot off the press. Stacy picked one up, the ink still fresh and slightly smudging her fingertips. The headlines screamed back at her: "The Torrential Terror Strikes Again" and "Hear No Evil: A City Gripped by Fear." A chill ran down her spine as she traced the bold letters with her eyes, knowing the power they wielded.

A mixture of excitement and dread washed over her. The story was no longer just words on a page. It had become a pulse, a heartbeat reverberating through St. Louis. By naming the monsters, the city would now brace for the storm they would bring.

WHEN THE FIRST COPIES BEGAN ROLLING OFF THE PRESS, A sense of foreboding clung to the ink. Stacy stood at the edge of the newsroom, her eyes fixated on the emerging newspapers. Her article was now immortalized in print and the enormity of her work whispered through the air. Her gut churned with equal parts pride and apprehension.

Outside, the sun struggled to break through gathering storm clouds, its pale light casting an eerie glow over the city. Newspaper readers would soon become familiar with the newly christened monsters that roamed among them. The names Stacy scripted would haunt their nightly dreams and daily lives. Amidst the media frenzy, she could sense the undercurrent of fear—every clap of thunder transforming into an omen, every whisper questioning who would be next.

Back in the cold light of her office, she grappled with the moral consequences of her sensationalism, questioning whether the urgency of informing the public justified the probable panic her words would incite.

Her thoughts drifted to the victims and their families. The pain was not abstract to them—it was visceral and unending. She wondered if her stories offered solace or merely deepened the wounds. She also considered her editor's perspective—he saw the paper's success in numbers and longevity, while Stacy battled with the line between journalistic duty and human empathy.

She braced against the edge of her desk, her knuckles pale and tight, and exhaled deeply. While the vibrant city braced itself against the impending storm and the horror of the killers now named, Stacy understood that each flash of insight she provided was a glimmer of light in the overshadowing gloom.

Staring into the horizon where the storm clouds gathered, she felt the press's first vibrations beneath her feet, echoing up through her bones. The story was out, along with a new wave of fear set loose upon St. Louis. Before leaving the building, her desk phone rang. It was her brother with some information he had learned from the streets. After several okays and a thank you, she hung up the phone and exited the building.

THE ENGINE OF STACY RHYMES' CAR PURRED AS SHE SPED through the streets of St. Louis, her mind racing faster than the vehicle she commanded. Gray clouds brewed ominously overhead, threatening another teeming downpour—the kind that seemed to bring out the city's underbelly. Her fingers gripped the steering wheel tightly as she navigated through traffic with calculated urgency. In her quest to uncover the Torrential Terror and Hear No Evil, each stoplight was an unwelcome delay. The city seemed to pulse with fear and uncertainty prompted by the deadly games of its hidden predators.

Finally reaching the police station, Stacy parked and hurried inside. The atmosphere was thick, filled with the chatter of officers and the buzz of scanners. She felt a momentary flash of trepidation but pushed it aside. This was her chance. Her footsteps echoed sharply as she made her way down the cold, gray hallway toward Mason Mind's cell.

Detective Alan Richardson stepped into Stacy's path and obstructed her determined pace. His piercing eyes did not blink. Their confrontation felt like a collision of wills. "You can't be here," he said, his voice an authoritative growl that brooked no argument.

Stacy's pulse quickened, not from fear but from her fiercely ingrained need to uncover the truth. "The public has a right to know," she retorted, squaring her shoulders. "And I have a right to do my job."

Richardson did not budge. "The public's right to know doesn't supersede the integrity of our investigation. Who gave you those details about the killings?"

Stacy's mind flashed through her past: the late nights spent chasing leads, the moments of triumph when she unmasked corruption, and the phone calls from her brother that had only fueled her fire for truth. She recalled her earlier conversations with Isaac Reynolds, Mason Mind's childhood friend turned LA Times reporter, whose cryptic hints had nudged her in the right direction. Even her editor's cautious optimism had instilled a sense of urgency.

Her jaw tightened as she prepared to defend her position. "My sources are confidential, and my work is protected by the First Amendment," she said, hoping her voice didn't betray her rising frustration. "Mason Mind might know something crucial. We can't afford to ignore any angle."

Richardson's stern gaze didn't waver, but there was a flicker of something—doubt, perhaps?—in his eyes. "You're meddling in something dangerous, Miss Rhymes," he warned. "Leave police work to the professionals."

The detective's words stung, but Stacy's resolve only strengthened. Her thoughts drifted to the victims—faces she had seen in the crime scene photos, frozen in their final moments of terror. Hear No Evil's unsettling signature haunted her; the frightful removal of ears spoke of a deep-seated cruelty she couldn't begin to fathom. The names she had given the killers carried the weight of their atrocities, and she felt an urgent responsibility to expose every layer of this grisly puzzle.

"Journalists are professionals too!" she shot back. "And sometimes, we're the only ones who can connect the dots."

Richardson sighed, a sound heavy with frustration and resignation. "Look, I get it. You're doing your job. But this isn't just another story, Stacy. People's lives depend on us getting this right."

"Do people's lives depend on you keeping secrets from the public?" she countered. The words felt heavy on her tongue, a blend of indignation and the fear of stepping over an unseen line. The weight of her own ambitions pressed down on her. Was she doing this for the story, the adrenaline rush of breaking news, or something deeper?

In that moment, she recalled previous stories that had changed laws, saved lives, and sometimes costed her more than a few sleepless nights. This was no different. The world needed to know the truth, even if the truth was buried beneath layers of bureaucracy and law enforcement bravado.

Richardson's face softened slightly, almost imperceptibly. "Stay out of police matters," he repeated, his voice low and dangerous. "That's your final warning."

Stacy met his gaze, a torrent of emotions swirling within her, yet she saw in the detective's eyes a mirror of her own stubbornness. He was also driven by a burning need for justice, but only through different means.

With a heavy heart, Stacy turned on her heel, Richardson's warning echoing in her ears. As she walked away, her thoughts were a tempest of frustration and resolve. The walls of the police station seemed to close in, a grim reminder of the barriers she constantly fought against. Each step took her further from Mason Mind and possibly closer to the truth she sought.

Outside, the sky had darkened further, and the first fat drops of rain began to fall, mirroring the heaviness in her chest. The city's fear was almost palpable, seeping through the cracks and shadows of its worn streets. But Stacy believed the truth was too critical to remain hidden and was thus undeterred. The stakes were too high.

She would find a way, despite the tempest and the emerging threats. For Stacy Rhymes, this was more than a story—it was a battle for justice, for the voices silenced by violence, and for the tenacity of uncovering what others wished to keep hidden. Her resolve grew stronger as she became increasingly soaked in the intensifying rain.

CHAPTER
TEN
THE PACT

In the dimly lit conference room, Mason and Isaac sat on the metal bench, the air heavy with unease. The soft hum of the lights in the background provided a semblance of normalcy, contrasting sharply with the tension that crackled between them. Mason's fingers traced the jagged edges of the metal tabletop as he mustered the courage to speak.

Mason began, "When I was a kid..." His voice was barely above a whisper: "I saw something..." He resumed after a pause, "horrible." His gaze dropped to the floor, avoiding Isaac's sympathetic eyes.

Isaac leaned in, his brows knitted in concern. "It's okay, Mason. I'm here. You can tell me."

Mason closed his eyes, the memory clawing its way to the forefront of his mind. He could still smell the tang of blood mixed with the earthy scent of wet leaves. He was eight years old, by his house behind a tree, his heart pounding in his chest. A girl's scream echoed through the woods, and he dared to look away.

"I saw a girl," he choked out, his voice trembling. "She was... she was having her eyes pulled out of her sockets." He finally looked at Isaac, his eyes wide with the terror of the remembered scene.

Isaac's face remained calm, a steady rock in the storm of Mason's emotions. "That's awful, Mason. I'm so sorry you had to see that."

Mason's breaths came in shallow gasps as he continued. "They accused me and some other boys of doing it, saying we were the ones who hurt her."

His mind raced back to the accusing faces, the whispers, and the pointed fingers. The adults had looked at him with a mixture of pity and suspicion, compounding his fear and confusion. How could they believe he was capable of such a thing? The weight of their words had pressed down on him, heavy like the storm clouds that often heralded his blackouts.

"I didn't do it, Isaac. I swear. But sometimes I wonder if they're right. What if there is something wrong with me?" Mason's voice cracked, and the admission of his deepest fear lay bare.

Isaac shook his head firmly. "You were just a kid, Mason. And you're not a monster. We know who the real monsters are: Torrential Terror and Hear No Evil. Not you."

Mason's heart ached with the turmoil of his emotions. Isaac's words were a balm, offering a glimmer of hope amid the chaos of his mind. The vivid recollection of the girl's vacant, hemorrhaging eyes haunted him, but Isaac's unwavering belief in his innocence provided a thin thread of stability.

"You believe me?" Mason asked, his voice barely audible.

"Of course I do," Isaac said firmly, his hand resting on Mason's shoulder. "We're going to figure this out. You're not alone in this."

Mason's eyes welled with tears as he nodded, the burden of his past slightly eased by Isaac's support. In the silence that followed, he felt a profound gratitude for having someone who didn't doubt him, even when he doubted himself.

As the minutes ticked by, they sat in reflective silence, the gravity of Mason's revelation settling between them. Isaac's presence was a silent promise of solidarity, a reminder that even in the face of unimaginable horror, friendship and compassion could offer a lifeline.

Mason's thoughts drifted to the broader context of his plight. The murderers had cast a shadow of dread over the entire community. Public opinion was a twisted, volatile entity, ready to latch onto any scapegoat to satiate its fear. The societal violence and distrust that had erupted were palpable, turning neighbor against neighbor and dividing the community into factions of suspicion and paranoia.

As Mason stared at the flickering shadows, he felt the smothering weight of being on the wrong side of public perception. His personal trauma was now intertwined with a larger narrative of terror and uncertainty. The community's desperation for answers could easily ensnare the innocent in its web of blame and vengeance.

Isaac, sensing Mason's wandering thoughts, spoke softly, breaking the silence. "We've known each other since we were kids, Mason. You've always been the one who saw beauty in the world, even when others couldn't. That hasn't changed. Don't let these nightmares steal that from you."

Their childhood friendship had matured into an enduring bond despite being tempered by dark experiences. Isaac's compassion was not just a comfort; it was a testament to their enduring connection, a lighthouse in Mason's stormy mind.

Mason turned to Isaac, his expression one of sincere appreciation. "Thank you, Isaac. For believing in me. For staying, even when things get... hard."

Isaac squeezed his shoulder gently. "That's what friends are for. We're in this together."

They sat quietly, their reflective silence a canvas for the complex emotions that swirled within Mason. Despite the dense, suffocating fear that clouded his memories, Isaac's unwavering presence cast a glimmer of light, however fragile, into his darkened world.

THE WOODS BEHIND THEIR CHILDHOOD HOMES TOWERED LIKE silent sentinels, dark branches reaching out like skeletal fingers in the night. Mason, Eric, and Isaac stood around a small makeshift fire; the flickering flames cast dancing shadows on their faces. The warmth of the firelight was a stark contrast to the chill in the air, mingling with the raw, unspoken emotions that hung heavy between them.

Eric broke the silence first, his voice steady but laden with an unspoken depth: "We've been through a lot together, and there's more to come. We need to make a blood pact. It's the only way to ensure that no matter what happens, we'll always be there for each other."

Mason's gaze, previously lost in the undulating flames, shifted to Eric. The memory of the girl's eyes being pulled out was vivid and replayed relentlessly like a film reel in his mind. He felt a visceral connection to the darkness surrounding them, the eerie quiet of the woods contrasting the turbulent storm within him.

Isaac, ever the steady rock, nodded in silent agreement. The firelight softened his features, yet his eyes reflected steadfast determination. He knew the significance of what Eric was proposing. The blood pact was more than just a promise; it was a declaration of their unbreakable bonds forged in the fires of shared trauma and a reality that kept testing their resolve.

Eric produced a small, sharp knife, its blade glinting ominously in the firelight. He held it out, his hand steady, his eyes unwavering. Taking a deep breath, he sliced his palm, the crimson blood welling up instantly. He then passed the knife to Isaac, who followed suit without hesitation. Finally, it came to Mason. His breath hitched as the steel touched his skin, the pain a simultaneous grounding sensation and a stark reminder of his reality's fragility.

One by one, they pressed their bleeding palms together, the mingling blood a symbol of their loyalty and commitment. The warmth of their shared blood seemed to momentarily stave off the chill of the night, binding them in a solemn promise. The crackling of the fire was the only sound, an eerie accompaniment to their unspoken vows.

Eric's voice broke the silence again, this time barely more than a whisper. "We're brothers now, bound by blood. No matter what the world throws at us, we're in this together."

Mason's grip tightened on theirs, drawing strength from their unity. His mind swirled with conflicting thoughts—fear, uncertainty, but also a flicker of hope. Their pact felt like a beacon in the darkness, a lifeline anchoring him to something solid and real.

Isaac took a moment to speak, his tone reflective and serious: "We've seen things tonight that most people can't even imagine. There's a storm around us, but we'll face it together. I believe in us, in this bond."

Each word echoed with sincerity, solidifying their commitment. The trauma Mason had revealed earlier was still fresh in their minds, but standing here, united by the fire and their blood, they felt an unspoken understanding strengthen their resolve.

As the firelight flickered and the woods closed in around them, they each silently made personal vows. Mason, haunted by his memories and fears, vowed to hold onto this moment of unity. Eric, the catalyst of their pact, promised to guide and protect them, supporting Mason's artistic dreams despite the chaos. Isaac, the steadfast supporter, pledged to be their rock, a constant source of strength and stability.

The moment hung heavy in the air, weighed with their shared histories and unspoken fears. The solemnity of their promise was palpable, its significance etched in their minds alongside the traumas they had endured. The fire before them reflected the intensity of their blood bond.

Finally, they released their grips, the fire reflecting in their eyes as they absorbed the gravity of their promise. The echoes of the past interlaced with their unspoken hopes for the future, creating a tapestry of emotion that bound them even tighter.

Eric, Mason, and Isaac stood in reflective silence, the crackle of the fire their only companion. Slowly, they began to make their way back to the house, their footsteps crunching softly on the forest floor, each step a quiet testament to the newfound strength they drew from their bond.

The significance of their pact lingered in the air, a silent promise that no matter the challenges ahead, they would face them together as brothers bound by blood and shared history.

ERIC, MASON, AND ISAAC STEPPED INTO THE FAMILIAR warmth of Eric's home, the heavy silence of their pact still echoing in the whispering darkness outside. The air within was thick with drying paint and turpentine, a creative sanctuary that stood in stark contrast to the turmoil in Mason's heart. The walls of Eric's studio, awash with canvases that told stories both grand and melancholic, seemed to breathe life into the room.

"Come here, Mason," Eric beckoned, his voice a blend of undeniable authority and deep affection. The studio was a cocoon of Eric's ambitions and dreams for his nephew, every inch of it dripping with the promise of a future where Mason could transform the chaos in his mind into captivating art.

Eric pointed to a chair, inviting Mason to sit. The chair creaked, embracing him as Eric began to speak. "Mason, you have a gift—a gift that needs to be seen by the world," he said as his eyes burned with conviction.

"I promise you, I will make sure you become the most famous painter ever. We'll show the world the beauty you can create."

The words were a lifeline into the abyss of Mason's doubts. His heart raced, a tumult of excitement and suffocating fear. Could he really be an artist renowned for his work, despite the whispers and glances that haunted him since the crime? Could he rise above the nightmares and the blackouts that threatened to consume his sanity?

Mason's gaze shifted to the canvases around him. Each painting, a fragment of his soul, mirrored his internal struggle. He remembered the child-like exuberance he felt when he first picked up a brush, the way colors danced on the canvas under his fingertips. But intertwined with those vibrant memories were the shadows of his blackouts, leaving him questioning his reality and his worth. He felt both the thrill of possibility and the weight of insecurity crashing against his mind.

Mason felt a twinge of hope as Eric outlined plans for gallery showings and exhibitions. His voice was a hopeful diorama of success. His uncle believed in him fiercely, a beacon cutting through the fog of his own inner torment. The conviction in Eric's eyes offered some semblance of stability in Mason's chaotic world. For a moment, he could almost see it clearly— his name revered in the art circles, his paintings cherished.

Isaac silently appeared at the doorway, wearing a supportive smile. He leaned against the frame, listening to Eric's impassioned speech about Mason's future. Isaac's presence was an omnipresent force of quiet strength. Since childhood, he had stood by Mason, a true ally navigating through the quagmires of life. Isaac had his own dreams of journalistic success, yet he never wavered in supporting Mason, even when the world cast its most unforgiving judgment on his friend.

"You've got this, Mason," Isaac said softly, his voice barely audible but heartening. Those few words were laden with sincerity, a promise of unwavering camaraderie. Isaac's belief intertwined with Eric's ambition, forming an unswervring coalition against Mason's self-doubt.

Mason's eyes lingered on one of his recent pieces—a tumultuous storm rendered with stark lines and chaotic splashes of color. The painting echoed his fear and confusion surrounding his blackouts. On thundering nights, those feelings were the most dreadfully intense. The art was not just an expression; it was his dialogue with his demons. Through the medium of paint, he untangled his torment and sought solace.

Eric's voice wove through Mason's thoughts, pulling him back. "You have a way of seeing the world in a kaleidoscope of coloration and shapes, which showcases your unique since of synesthesia. The ability to evoke such profound emotion is rare. Don't let anyone, especially those who doubt you because of these horrific events, take that away from you."

The room thickened with the scent of oils and the palpable bond between them. Within these walls, beneath Eric's unwavering gaze and Isaac's silent fortitude, Mason felt an ember of confidence ignite. The oppressive atmosphere that had followed him like a shadow began to lift, replaced by a fragile yet growing determination to reclaim his identity.

Eric's studio was more than a safe space; it was a crucible of transformation. As Mason sat there, absorbing his uncle's words, he started to believe in a future where his art could transcend his nightmares. Where truths, both light and dark, could be conveyed through canvas.

Eric clasped Mason's shoulder firmly, planting a seed of hope. "We're in this together, no matter what. You will achieve greatness."

Mason glanced at Isaac, who gave a nod of encouragement. A silent understanding passed among them. Theirs was an uncertain path, but together, they could navigate it.

In that moment of unity, with the faint hope sparking in his chest, Mason's eyes returned to his artwork. Each brushstroke now seemed to shimmer with potential. For the first time, he dared to imagine a future where he was not entrapped by his past or tethered by his fears. Surrounded by the canvases that bore his soul, supported by the resolute figures of Eric and Isaac, Mason allowed himself to hope, if only for a fleeting moment. And in that ephemeral glimmer, a newfound resolve took root.

CHAPTER
ELEVEN
THE PAST

D etective Alan Richardson stepped through the large, double glass doors of the STLPD headquarters. The early morning sun rays that managed to filter through the city's overcast, made long shadows across the precinct's lobby. The bustle of early shifts and the murmured conversations of officers filled the air, mingling with the hum of electronics and the occasional ring of telephones.

Richardson moved with purpose, his eyes set, his jaw clenched. He had barely slept the night before, thoughts of Mason Mind's enigmatic past and the impending threats of the current serial killers plaguing his every moment. Detective Matthews met him near the central briefing area, a thick folder in hand.

"Morning, Alan," Matthews greeted tersely, his expression mirroring the gravity of the situation. "We have some new intel on Mason. His past is more twisted than we thought."

Richardson nodded, taking the proffered folder. His fingers brushed against the rough edges of the papers, stinging slightly—a tactile reminder that every detail counted. "Let's go somewhere we can discuss this privately," he said, beckoning Matthews to follow.

They shuffled into a vacant conference room, the door closing with a soft click. Matthews wasted no time, diving right into the briefing. "We've uncovered records suggesting a significant trauma from Mason's childhood. Attached here," he tapped the folder, "are detailed reports, including one incident involving his eye socket. It appears his childhood was marked by more than one gruesome event."

Richardson opened the folder, his eyes scanning the pages quickly but thoroughly. Newspaper clippings, psychological evaluations, and personal notes created a grim mosaic of a troubled youth. He thought back to previous cases, where childhood traumas had festered, corrupted, and become adulthood seeds that blossomed into something sinister.

"How did this stay buried for so long?" Richardson asked. His voice reflected a mix of frustration and urgency.

"Fragmented records and shifting foster homes—he slipped through the cracks," Matthews replied while leaning against the conference table. "It's essential we dig deeper, Alan. There's something here that might explain his blackouts and perhaps even exonerate him."

Richardson tightened his grip on the folder. He felt a pang of empathy for Mason, imagining the horrors the boy must have faced—an artist now, but once, merely a child caught in the web of fate. Richardson's own past crowded into his thoughts of cases where victims had been failed by the very system designed to protect them. The echoes of those unsolved crimes gnawed at him, fueling his determination.

With a resolute nod, he decided on the next course of action. "We need to trace every step of Mason's life. Get his full historical records from the archives department—birth, school, medical, psychological—everything."

Matthews gave a curt nod and exited the room, leaving Richardson alone with his thoughts. He visualized Mason not as a suspect but as a boy molded by unrelenting trauma. The sensation of his pulse quickening echoed the sense of urgency throbbing in his veins.

By mid-morning, the archives department delivered a stack of records. Richardson sifted through the files in his office, each document a portal into Mason's troubled past. Reports of the eye socket incident stood out starkly. He recalled the specifics from an earlier incident in vivid flashes; he saw a young Mason lying in a sterile hospital bed, tears mixed with blood, eyes raw with pain and confusion.

The grim details pushed Richardson to accept that Mason's psyche was shaped by childhood trauma. As he perused the papers, Richardson wondered silently about the connection between these blackouts and the serial killings. The pattern was far from clear. However, threads were there and they were waiting to be unraveled.

Another memory interrupted his thoughts—one of his own past cases, where unnoticed scars had driven a man to desperate acts. Based on that experience, Richardson promised himself never to overlook the hidden wounds that shape human behavior. He felt the weight of that promise now more than ever.

Rising from his chair, he knew what came next. He needed to talk to people who had known Mason to gather firsthand accounts of his past. There were too many gaps, and too many shadows lurking behind the facade of the man Mason had become.

As he breathed in the slightly stale air of his office, Richardson made a decision. He was not just unveiling the truth for Mason; he was fighting against another potential miscarriage of justice. He couldn't let this case go cold; he couldn't let those silent screams of neglected childhood ghosts go unheard.

He left his office to inform Matthews and the Chief of his new plan. "I'll start interviews today," he said, urgently coloring his tone. "We need to speak to everyone who remembers Mason from his school days and his neighborhood—anyone who saw the cracks forming."

With renewed determination, Richardson set off to unearth the truth. He vowed to himself and the city he would leave no stone unturned as he excavated layers of obscured memories and societal neglect. He was prepared to confront the deep shadows of the past. He was ready to confront them. He was ready to shine a light on the darkness that had haunted Mason Mind for far too long.

THE EARLY MORNING RAYS FILTERED THROUGH THE TALL windows of Mason's former school, casting shadows across the tiled floor. Detective Alan Richardson walked briskly through the hallways, his polished shoes echoing with each step. The faint smell of old chalk and disinfectant filled the air, accompanied by the murmur of distant conversations among staff.

He arrived at the principal's office and knocked lightly on the door. Principal Dr. Breana Kirkland, a woman in her late fifties with silver-streaked hair and kind but weary eyes, greeted him. She ushered him inside with a gesture of her hand.

"Thank you for seeing me on such short notice, Dr. Kirkland," Richardson began, settling into a worn leather chair.

Dr. Kirkland sat across from him, her hands resting on a stack of faded yearbooks. "Of course, Detective. I was the principal here during Mason Mind's time. How can I assist?"

Detective Richardson leaned forward, his eyes intent. "Mason Mind suffered a traumatic incident involving his eyes when he was a child. I need to understand how that incident impacted him."

Dr. Kirkland sighed deeply, her eyes clouded with the weight of difficult memories. "Mason was in third grade when it happened. He was a curious, bright boy with an extraordinary talent for art, but after the eye socket incident," she paused before resuming, "he changed."

She then retrieved an old folder with Mason's name. "Mason became withdrawn. He isolated himself during recess, no longer engaging in the games he once loved. His art, however, grew darker, more abstract. He poured his pain into his sketches and paintings, but he stopped sharing them with anyone."

Richardson took notes, his pen scratching against the paper. "And his interaction with others? Friends? Teachers?"

"Around the same time, he began losing friends. They couldn't understand what he was going through, and he wouldn't let them in. His teachers noticed as well. Mason would sit at the back of the class, doodling in his notebook instead of participating. We were all very concerned, but he rebuffed any attempts to help."

Dr. Kirkland chuckled sadly. "There was one time—I remember it clearly. We had an art contest, and Mason submitted a piece that stunned us all. It was a haunting, intricate drawing of an eye, filled with raw emotion. His talent was undeniable, but so was his pain."

Detective Richardson absorbed her words, pondering the critical moments that had reshaped Mason's young life. After thanking Dr. Kirkland, he left the school and navigated through the nearby neighborhood where Mason grew up.

The neighborhood, though aged, still held remnants of its once vibrant community. Children's laughter occasionally punctuated the morning serenity, and the smell of fresh-cut grass mingled with the slight pungency of car exhaust. Richardson approached an elderly woman tending to her garden. Her eyes crinkled in recognition as he introduced himself.

"Ah, Mason Mind," she said with nostalgia tinging her voice. "A quiet boy, always with his sketchpad. He'd sit on that park bench over there for hours, capturing the world with his pencils."

Another neighbor, a middle-aged man walking his dog, joined the conversation. "Mason was always polite. His drawings were something special. But after that incident..." He shook his head. "Well, he wasn't the same. Became almost invisible. People started talking, suspecting things. Some of them still do."

Richardson pressed on, asking probing questions that brought forth more fragmented memories. One elderly man described how Mason once painted a mural for a community event—a beautiful scene of the park that captured its essence flawlessly. "He had a gift, that boy. But gifts can be heavy burdens, can't they?"

The detective noted the sadness in their voices, an undercurrent of something lost. Their recollections painted a picture of a community that had seen Mason both as a beacon of potential and as a victim of unspoken fears.

As Richardson walked back towards his car, he was deep in thought. The connections between Mason's childhood trauma, his artistic expressions, and his current predicament were becoming clearer. He understood that the scars left by that terrible day in Mason's youth had extended far beyond the physical, seeping into his psyche, steering his path to the present darkness.

With the neighborhood's stories echoing in his mind, Richardson considered his next steps. The key to solving the case was recognizing Mason's trauma and blackouts were interwoven. This insight fortified Richardson's commitment to uncovering the truth. No matter how deeply it was buried in the recesses of Mason's tortured memories.

DETECTIVE ALAN RICHARDSON STRODE INTO THE STLPD headquarters, the morning sun casting long shadows through the glass doors. His mind buzzed with the labyrinth of clues he had unraveled, each tangled thread leading back to Mason Mind's enigmatic past. Detective Matthews was already waiting in the dimly lit briefing room, eyes sharp and demeanor brisk.

"Matthews, we need to talk," Richardson said, his voice a rugged whisper of urgency.

Matthews flicked through a stack of papers. "I've gone through what you found this morning. Mason's past... it's a minefield of trauma."

As Richardson relayed the grim details of his investigation, Matthews listened intently, nodding at intervals. The mere mention of Mason's childhood trauma, specifically the eye socket incident, seemed to cast a pall over the room.

"The principal described him as withdrawn and troubled after the incident," Richardson continued. "Couple that with the fact everyone in his neighborhood remembers him as a quiet artist... It's starting to form a picture, but it's still hazy."

The chief entered, his imposing presence filling the space with an air of authority. Richardson turned to brief him, recounting the troubling findings with methodical precision. The chief's eyes narrowed with concern.

"We need to reassess Mason Mind's psychological evaluations," the chief interjected. "There could be links between his trauma and these blackouts. If we don't explore this further, we might miss something crucial."

Richardson's thoughts raced. Mason's blackouts were as shrouded in mystery as the killings themselves. Each blackout was a haunting void, and in those voids, horrors might emerge, horrors hidden from his own conscious mind. The pressing fear of Mason's innocence or guilt hung over Richardson like a storm cloud, ready to unleash havoc on everyone involved.

The chief's suggestion was not just a prudent step; it was a lifeline to sanity amidst the chaos. "I'll call Mason's psychiatrist," Richardson said, his voice tense with the weight of responsibility.

Moments later, Richardson found himself in the eggshell white office of Dr. Amora Tillman, a woman whose calm exterior belied the turbulent complexities she navigated as a psychiatrist.

"Detective," she greeted, her eyes studying Richardson with professional detachment. They sat across from one another, the oppressive stillness of the room amplifying Richardson's simmering anxiety.

He cut to the chase. "Dr. Tillman, I need to understand Mason Mind's psychological state. Specifically, I'm interested in the connection between his blackouts and the killings we're investigating."

Dr. Tillman paused and cleared her throat, "You know what you are asking me to answer is unethical. I have a sworn duty to my patients and my medical practice. For the safety sake of the City of St. Louis, I need you to ask me questions indirectly to my patient, but in a sense that I can answer in general without incriminating myself or my profession."

With a smirk on his face, he understood that this conversation was going to be cryptic. "How can we connect a person's blackouts with possible killings?"

Dr. Tillman leaned back slightly, fingers interlaced over her lap. "A person's blackouts can be closely tied to their traumatic experiences from childhood. Possibly having incidents more than a physical trauma. And possibly have a psyche retreated from the event, creating these blackouts as a defense mechanism."

Richardson absorbed her words, his mind flashing to the chilling patterns he'd seen in the murders. Each kill felt methodical yet equally chaotic—much like Mason's artwork, which could swing from serene landscapes to violent abstractions. Was it possible that within those black-outs, another persona was at play, carrying out these sinister acts?

"Are you saying one could be committing these crimes without aware-ness?" Richardson's voice was edged with a rare tremor, the gravity of his question hanging in the air.

"It's possible," Dr. Tillman confirmed. "The brain has ways of compartmentalizing trauma, creating separate identities or states to cope with unbearable pain. If that person is your killer, he might genuinely have no recollection."

The dread gnawed at Richardson's insides. If Mason was indeed the Torrential Terror, it meant he was a man trapped by his own mind. He was a prisoner of past horrors manifesting into present brutality. But what if he wasn't? The doubt added layers to Richardson's already complex senti-ments—an artist he had respected and now had to dissect like an emotion-less puzzle.

"Detective, their episodes can be triggered by intense emotional strife," Dr. Tillman added. "Their blackouts can be aligned with the timing of the murders, but to link them definitively, you would need more than psychological patterns. You would need concrete evidence."

Richardson' reflected on other unsolved cases with these unsettling similarities. Patterns of killers with trauma-induced psychoses weren't unheard of. But never had they been interwoven so tightly with the fabric of someone's artistic genius—a genius that he once admired. Now, that same talent might be a mask for the grotesque.

He was beginning to feel overwhelmed with a sense of impending catastrophe along with his own past's burdens. Every unsolved case flashed before his eyes like phantom specters of his failings. The memories accused him of his previous failures to catch the real criminal before more lives were lost. The community's safety hung in the balance, as did his own professional integrity.

"Thank you, Dr. Tillman. You've given me a lot to think about," Richardson said, his tone caught between gratitude and resignation.

Leaving the psychiatrist's office, doubt and determination conjured a maelstrom in his mind. He was aware that every second wasted pushed them closer to another potential tragedy.

His resolve solidified with each step. He would dig deeper, unfurl every hidden corner of Mason's mind, and prevent the specter of his past from casting a lethal shadow on the present. The truth lay somewhere in the maze of Mason's psyche, and Richardson would not rest until he unearthed it.

DETECTIVE ALAN RICHARDSON SAT HUNCHED OVER THE cluttered desk in his dimly lit office, the weight of years of unsolved cases pressing onto his shoulders. The late afternoon sun cast long shadows through the blinds, slicing the room into fragments of light and dark. The murmur of activity from the STLPD headquarters outside his door felt distant, muffled by the chaos inside his mind.

He flipped through the pages of Mason Mind's file, the rustle of paper a whisper in the oppressive silence. While scanning for familiar words, his attention was snagged by a phrase written in bold: unsolved cases. Images surged in his mind like a rushing river breaching its banks, submerging him in memories he'd rather forget.

The Subzero case. It had been two years since that nightmare ended. Or rather, it did not end because it was never truly resolved. The thoughts of the FBI investigation that became a noose around his neck returned with vengeance along with memories of the suffocating pressure of unmet expectations and lingering doubts. He could still feel the icy tension in the room where he and the other agents had gathered, their distrust as palpable as the cold steel of their service pistols.

Back in the FBI office, the suspicion had oozed through every interaction. Had he done enough? Could he have stopped it? They'd eyed him like he was the mole, the one who had slipped up and let the killer vanish into the fog. Richardson clenched his jaw, the muscles working furiously as he remembered the almost inaudible whispers, the sideways glances that said more than words ever could.

He squeezed his eyes shut, trying to block out the interrogation room where he had to repeatedly defend himself against colleagues who were almost more hostile than the criminals they hunted. Nights of insomnia had become routine; he had lain awake, haunted by visions of unsolved cases piling atop his chest like bodies in a shallow grave, each one a testament to his supposed failures.

Opening his eyes, Richardson's gaze fell back onto Mason's file. His thoughts flickered to the blackouts Mason experienced, the eerie parallels that resonated disturbingly with his own lapses in confidence. The pressures of their respective pasts created a bridge between the detective and the accused—a bridge built on the shaky foundations of trauma and unresolved mysteries.

He thought of Agent Jones, always poker-faced but with eyes that betrayed every suspicion. Their professional relationship had never recovered from Subzero's aftermath. The unspoken accusations and icy formalities replaced the camaraderie they might have once shared. In his isolated quest for truth, Richardson often found himself in adversarial stances where allies should have stood.

As he dwelled on these thoughts, Richardson felt a mounting anxiety, a gnawing dread that history might repeat itself. He could not let Torrential Terror and Hear No Evil slip through his grasp as Subzero did. The urgency intensified with every heartbeat, the pulse in his veins echoing the tick of a clock counting down to another failure. The public's watchful eyes and the relentless media frenzy—each carving further into his resilience.

He shuffled the pages restlessly, his fingers trembling slightly. Memories flooded his mind—a torrent of unresolved cases, each a scar on his psyche. He recalled the victims' faces, the families' tears, and the bitter taste of promises unfulfilled. He remembered the sleepless nights, wandering the labyrinth of his mind, desperate to piece together puzzle fragments that eluded him.

The psychological debris from Subzero lingered, like the fog in a nightmare that blurs the boundary between reality and delusion. He needed to redeem himself, to exorcise the demons of guilt and regret that tormented him. Every unresolved case was a ghost that haunted the halls of his soul, echoing through the corridors of his memories.

Richardson rose from his chair, his silhouette stark against the dimming light. Determination surged within him, a ferocious resolve to crack the enigma of the current killings. Another failed case was not an option. The faces of the victims from his current cases melded with those from Subzero, a appalling gallery urging him forward.

He muttered to himself, low and fierce, voicing a promise forged in desperation and steel. "Not this time." His vow echoed in the stillness, a declaration against the abyss threatening to consume him. He couldn't afford another unsolved case, another question mark hanging over his career—the specter of failure lurking everywhere.

With renewed focus, Richardson returned to the files. He focused upon each word as if they were threads in a tapestry he was determined to unravel. The labyrinth would not defeat him this time. He would find the key, unveil the truth, and bring the Torrential Terror and Hear No Evil to justice.

He flipped through the reports, scanning connections and patterns with an intensity that bordered on obsession. The relentless pursuit of answers became his mantra, a mental balm against the mounting pressure. As he pieced together the fragments of Mason's fractured past, the bigger picture started to form—hazy yet promising.

His fingers danced over Mason's records with a surgical precision, peeling back the layers of trauma and truth. The night beckoned, filled with unanswered questions and the whispers of those long silenced. As the sun dipped below the horizon, Richardson felt the weight of his vow settle into his bones.

He would solve this. He had to.

DETECTIVE ALAN RICHARDSON STOOD AT THE HEAD OF THE conference room, his eyes scanning the familiar faces seated around the table. The weight of the current crisis bore heavily on him, etched in the stern lines of his face. The overhead fluorescent lights buzzed slightly, casting a cold, clinical pallor over the room. A grim collage of despair consisting of crime scene photos, maps, and other files was strewn across the table.

"Let's get started," Richardson said, his voice gravelly from a day filled with many questions and few answers. He tapped a stack of papers against the table, organizing his thoughts as much as the documents.

Detective Matthews leaned back slightly in his chair, the self-doubt evident in the lines around his eyes. Having worked with Richardson for years, he both admired and resented the former FBI agent's unyielding determination. Matthews couldn't help but feel a constant, gnawing sense of inadequacy, wondering if he would ever measure up.

"Based on our investigations, there's a clear connection between the current serial killings and Mason's past trauma," Richardson began. His gaze briefly met Matthews, acknowledging the tension beneath their professional veneer. "We need to understand these connections better if we're going to stop the Torrential Terror and Hear No Evil."

Agent Jones, sitting across from Matthews, leaned forward, a calculated glint in his eye. "I've been thinking," he said, his voice measured and deliberate. "We might need to broaden our search parameters. Look into other unsolved cases that could link back to Subzero. There might be patterns we've missed."

Richardson nodded, appreciating Jones' strategic mind. They had worked together before, though never this closely. There was mutual respect but also an unspoken competitive edge. Each man is driven by his own set of unrelenting standards. Jones' suggestion didn't surprise Richardson; the agent was known for his methodical, all-encompassing approach.

Lt. Lisa Rozzoro, head of the forensic lab, interjected with a note of caution. "If we're expanding our parameters, we need to ensure our team is not spread too thin. We've already got enough on our plate, and every misstep brings us closer to another victim." Her pragmatic nature often served as a stabilizing force amidst the chaos, her insights a blend of scientific rigor and grounded realism.

Sitting beside Lt. Rozzoro, Sgt. Anderson shifted uncomfortably. The gravity of recent events weighed heavily on him, the brutal images of crime scenes flashing in his mind. Despite the tension, he couldn't deny a growing respect for Richardson's unflagging resolve. "We need an action plan," Sgt. Anderson said, his voice firm despite his nerves. "Something concrete to guide us through the night."

Richardson took a deep breath, feeling the enormity of the task ahead. The room pulsed with a mixture of urgency and unvoiced fears. "Our primary objective is to profile the locations where these killings have occurred and identify potential new targets. Based on Mason's movements and the killer's patterns, we have several hot spots we need to cover."

Maplewood, Clayton, and Ladue—neighborhood names circled in red ink—were stark contrasts against the whiteboard beside him. Places where the scent of rain had signaled death, where terror spread through swarming downpours.

Isaac Reynolds, the LA Times reporter and erstwhile friend of Mason Mind, watched quietly from a corner, his presence a reminder of the potential media blowback if they failed. His loyalty to Mason was unquestionable, but as a journalist, he couldn't afford to ignore the tangible tensions tethering the room's air.

Agent Jones spoke up again, a trace of urgency in his voice. "We should also move beyond just geographical markers. Psychological profiling of the killers and understanding their triggers might lead us to predictive behavioral patterns."

The team nodded, a collective hum of agreement washing over the table. Seconds ticked by, heavy with the weight of impending danger and the haunting realization of the stakes involved. Within the walls of STLPD headquarters, fear mingled with determination, creating a volatile undercurrent that could either galvanize or fracture them.

Richardson rubbed his temples, feeling the weariness seep into his bones. His thoughts drifted momentarily to Subzero, the cold case that had marked him as both a prodigy and a pariah among his peers. The frustration of that unresolved horror gnawed at him still, a constant specter that haunted his sleepless nights.

"We split into teams," Richardson finally said, his voice cutting through the tension. His eyes bore into each member, imprinting his resolve onto theirs. "We cross-reference Mason's history with current patterns of attacks. Detectives Matthews and Sgt. Anderson, you cover Maplewood. Agent Jones and Lt. Rozzoro, take Clayton. I'll handle Ladue." He pushed the papers toward his teammates. Each file was a potential key or dead end.

As they reviewed their next steps, Richardson glanced around the room. Trust, fragile and fraught, connected them all. Yet beneath the surface, doubts churned, insecurities lingered, and past grievances weighed like unseen shackles. They would either find their coherence in these challenging moments or risk further division.

Their final moments in the conference room were punctuated by the distant rumble of thunder, a grim reminder of the tormenting presence outside. With their plan set, the team moved purposefully, each step echoing a tacit agreement: whatever came next, they would confront it together, as fragmented as they might be.

CHAPTER
TWELVE
SERENDIPITOUS

Detective Alan Richardson's desk was a chaotic jumble of files and papers, a visual testament to the myriad cases he had juggled during his career. The gentle hum of fluorescent lights buzzed overhead, casting long shadows across the precinct that seemed almost tangible in the late afternoon haze. The sanctity of his focus was broken by the sudden ringing of the phone. Its shrill tone cut through the office noise like a knife.

"Richardson here," he answered, his voice gruff but professional.

"Detective, it's Stacy Rhymes," came the voice on the other end. "I've got something you might want to look into. There's been some unusual activity around a property owned by Jason Falls."

Richardson's interest immediately piqued at the mention of Jason Falls. Falls had always been a person of interest in their ongoing investigations, and any lead connected to him warranted immediate attention. He jotted down a quick note and leaned back in his chair, the leather creaking under his weight.

"Tell me everything you know, Stacy," he said, leaning forward, the urgency in his voice thinly veiled.

"Neighbors have reported strange deliveries, and there's evidence of heavy foot traffic late at night," Stacy replied, her tone precise and urgent.

"It's a dilapidated neighborhood. Falls' property sticks out—practically a fortress compared to the surrounding decay."

"Got it. Thanks for the tip, Stacy. I'll check it out," Richardson said, ending the call and immediately turning to his computer to pull up records related to Falls. The digital screen flickered with rows of data, confirming the address and detailing a litany of previous suspicions— nothing conclusive, but enough to bolster his resolve. That's why no hits, the computer has Jason parent's address listed. How did Stacy get this other address?

He allowed himself a moment to reflect. Bureaucracy had always been a hurdle, a constant battle against red tape and protocol. Some procedural technicalities had caused a few cases to slip through his fingers. Which contributed to the gnawing frustration that came with the territory of chasing shadows, especially the sinister ones cast by The Torrential Terror and Hear No Evil.

Putting those thoughts aside, Richardson grabbed his jacket and keys. Outside, the low sun cast long, eerie shadows that seemed to stretch endlessly, mirroring the sinister undertones of the investigation. He got into his car, and fastened the seatbelt with a determined snap. The engine growled to life as Richardson navigated his way through the winding streets of the city, his eyes scanning for any sign of the dilapidated neighborhood Stacy had mentioned.

Arriving at the location, a wave of familiarity mixed with dread washed over him. The neighborhood was a picture of decay; crumbling facades of houses lined the streets, their windows like empty eyes staring into nothingness. The air was thick with the smell of damp and rotten.

Richardson parked his car a block away and walked the rest of the distance, noting the details Stacy had described. Jason Falls' property was indeed incongruous with its surroundings. Whereas other houses bore the marks of neglect, sagging porches, and overgrown lawns, Falls' stood tall and intimidating, its appearance reinforced by barred windows and high fences.

This place, with its stark contrast to the surrounding decrepitude, felt like a rotting tooth in an otherwise decaying mouth. Alan circled the perimeter, noting the lack of activity at this hour. He could almost hear the whispers of its secrets, buried deep within its walls.

Returning to his car, Richardson pulled out his notes and meticulously recorded his observations. His mind churned with possible connections, each more troubling than the last. The eeriness of the location echoed previous hideous discoveries, and his instincts screamed that this was more than just a haven for a criminal—this was a lair for a predator. The pervasive sense of dread seemed to coil tighter around him, amplifying the stakes of his investigation.

Filing his notes, he resolved to visit the property in person with a backup plan and reinforcements. Years on the job had taught him that caution was paramount. The comparison to prior cases had weighed heavily upon him, highlighting the disturbing similarities and the potential horrors lying in wait.

As Richardson gathered his belongings, preparing to return to the precinct, his thoughts slipped back to the looming pressures of his exacting job. This case, with all of its twisted, labyrinthine connections, was pushing him to the edge. His mind whirred with the implications of his next steps; the path before him vanished into an opaque fog of uncertainty.

He flicked off the car's interior light, the darkness swallowing him briefly before the engine roared back to life, and he slowly drove away, the property now just a grim silhouette in his rearview mirror. The sun dipped further below the horizon, casting the world in a dim twilight that seemed almost unnatural, a prelude to the chilling events yet to come.

THE FLUORESCENT LIGHTS OVERHEAD BUZZED FAINTLY AS THE officer behind the front desk leafed through a stack of reports. Monotonous silence filled the lobby, the clock ticking loudly. The routine of the police station was shattered when a UPS delivery driver entered. With his eyes shadowed under his cap's brim, Jason Fall handed over a weighty package wrapped in plain brown paper. The desk officer, Sgt. Henderson, barely glanced up, his mind occupied with the day's tedium.

"Sign here," Jason murmured, an eerie casualness in his tone. Henderson scribbled his name, nodding distractedly as the driver disappeared into the evening.

Without giving it much thought, Henderson sliced the tape and unfolded the package. The room slipped into a slow-motion nightmare as he lifted the flaps. Blood drained from his face, his eyes widening in visceral horror. Inside the box, nestled among packing peanuts, sat a human head, eyes lifeless and mouth agape in a final scream.

A blood-curdling scream of disbelief escaped Henderson, echoing off the sterile walls. His body trembled, the grisly sight searing into his memory. Chaos erupted. Officers rushed to the desk, their reactions a whirlwind of shock and panic.

"What the hell is going on?" Matthews barked, his voice cutting through the cacophony. He stepped closer, his eyes bulging as he saw the monstrous content.

"Chief, Richardson, get here now!" An officer yelled into the radio, urgency thick in his voice. The panic splintered into pieces of frantic activity. The lobby became a storm of activity as phones rang, orders were barked, and officers scrambled to secure the area.

Tension crackled through the air. Henderson felt himself swelling with a desperate need to regain control. "Lock it down! Lock everything down!" he roared, forcing steel into his voice. His eyes scanned the faces of his colleagues, noting the terror reflecting his own.

The chief stormed into the lobby, a growl of authority under the cacophony. "Seal the premises. No one comes in or out until we figure out what the hell this is," he commanded. Officers moved swiftly, heels clicking a staccato of efficiency against the tiles, each one grappling with their rising dread in their own way.

Det. Richardson burst through the doors, his presence a cold wind of resolve. The scene met him like a punch to the gut. Officers milled about in chaos, their voices a jumble of frantic, clipped sentences. The atmosphere thickened with an undercurrent of fear, a collective pulse that threatened to overwhelm the room.

"Make a hole!" Richardson's voice cut sharply, slicing through panic like a blade. He strode forward with determination, exuding a calm that belied the rising tide of horror.

The forensic team arrived, their equipment wheeled in on carts. Richardson's eyes met the lead forensic officer, Lt. Rozzoro. A silent understanding passed between them, a nod toward their shared mission. The team set to work with surgical precision, cataloging the grotesque artifact. The oppressive weight of the moment settled over everyone, each officer acutely aware of the stakes.

Richardson scanned the room, reading the subtle signs of his colleagues' unraveling nerves. Matthews' hands clenched into white knuckled fists, his anger barely contained beneath the surface. Sgt. Anderson, a veteran of too many horrors, stood still, his face a mask of grim acceptance. Simone White, ever the skeptic, muttered nervously, a faint attempt at grounding herself in the familiarity of procedure.

"Everyone focus!" Richardson's command was met with a tight nod from the team. He peered into the box, his stomach lurching but his mind sharpening like a razor's edge on the task. Every detail could crack this case open.

As the forensics team worked, Richardson took a step back, his mind racing. The presentation of the head was a sickening signature. It was a taunt, a sinister message meant to unnerve them and elevate the stakes in this twisted game. His thoughts echoed back to the profile he'd built— methodical, deeply disturbed, a perpetrator who reveled in fear.

The room buzzed with tension, officers working frenetically to maintain some semblance of order. Their clipped dialogue revealed their struggles to grapple with the horror laid before them.

"Who the hell even... How did this—" one officer stammered, his voice cracking.

"Focus on securing the scene!" Another snapped, attempting to corral their collective dread into action.

Richardson caught a few nervous exchanges between junior officers— whispers of disbelief and macabre humor—betraying their rookie status. Scenes like this would blaze permanent scars onto their memories. Under their veneer of professionalism lay raw humanity, a collective vulnerability laid bare.

As the minutes stretched, he stood rooted in the chaos, the weight of the city's fear, and the impending storm of media scrutiny pressing heavily on his shoulders. Richardson's thoughts swirled with potential connections, possibilities thick with dread. This grotesque delivery, this severed head, was more than a simple message—it was a promise of what was to come.

He looked around at his team, their faces etched with horror, determination, and disbelief. They had seen death, but this was a mockery of life's sanctity, a deliberate ploy to instill fear. There was no time for their doubt.

Only by working together could they crack the code of this heinous act before more bodies appeared.

His voice rang out clear and steady, anchoring them all in the frantic sea. "This is just the beginning. We don't let this break us. We get ahead of it. Understand?"

A collective nod welcomed him, their resolve hardening under his gaze. They were professionals—scarred, yes, but not broken. They would face the storm raging outside and within, standing firm in the face of death's taunts.

With the forensics team engrossed in their work and the officers now methodically executing orders, Richardson took a deep breath, steeling himself for the next unrelenting step in this nightmare. The city's safety depended on their every move, and he had no intention of letting terror win.

Det. Richardson observed the chaos around him one last time, his eyes narrowing with fierce determination. This was more than a case; it was a battle against the encroaching abyss.

DETECTIVE ALAN RICHARDSON GLANCED AT THE CLOCK ON HIS desk, then at the hastily assembled SWAT team waiting for orders. The station buzzed with the weight of the evening's recent events, tension hanging thick in the air. The discovery of the severed head was a grim precursor, a frightening invitation to the nightmare that awaited them.

Richardson's fingers flicked through the files on Jason Falls, the name now etched into his memory. The neighborhood surrounding Falls's house had long been a breeding ground for unease, its crumbling facades and flickering streetlights standing like silent witnesses to countless unsolved crimes. Each broken window and graffitied wall whispered tales of betrayals and bloodshed.

"All right, listen up," Richardson's voice cut through the chatter. "We've got a short window to move in. Falls's house is our target. We have reasons to believe he's our man—part of the horrifying duo haunting our city."

As he laid out the plan, he couldn't help but think of the anxious eyes peering from behind closed curtains, the worried faces of families who had lost loved ones to senseless violence. The hell at Jason Falls's property was a festering wound, and tonight they aimed to cut it out.

The SWAT team, dressed in black tactical gear, moved with precision. Richardson led the convoy through the winding, dimly lit streets. The neighborhood around them seemed to close in, the suffocating gloom giving way to the eerie brilliance of their headlights. Alan's mind replayed every piece of evidence, every lead that had drawn them to this night.

They arrived in front of Falls's house, an old, nearly abandoned building that lurked in the shadow of an overgrown maple tree. The house sat in a derelict part of the city, its neighboring structures long abandoned, their hollow windows like empty eye sockets watching the approaching force. This area had once thrived, but now it subsisted with a haunted emptiness, a stark reminder of lives disrupted by fear and loss.

Richardson signaled to the team, and within moments, they spread out, surrounding the decrepit property. He drew his weapon, its cold steel giving him a sense of focus, a brutal tether to the reality of the situation.

"On my count," he whispered into the radio, his eyes scanning every window, every possible threat. The silence was palpable, more oppressive than the murmuring wind. "Three... two... one... breach!"

The battering ram made a thunderous announcement of their arrival as the front door splintered under its force. The team flooded into the house, their movements choreographed with military precision. Richardson's senses heightened; every creak of the floor, every shadow, became a potential threat.

"Clear the rooms," Richardson barked, adrenaline sharpening his commands. Each room they passed through painted a disturbing picture of Jason Falls's existence. Faded wallpaper clung stubbornly to the walls, and debris littered the floor, a testament to years of neglect and hidden horrors.

The basement door jutted, slightly ajar, a gateway to the underbelly of this hellish abode. Richardson motioned for a couple of officers to follow. As they descended the narrow, creaking staircase, the air grew colder, thicker, as if tainted by the unspeakable acts committed down here.

At the bottom, the beam of his flashlight illuminated a repugnant sight. Sprawled across the cold concrete floor were bodies and what remained of them, grotesquely arranged like puppets in a heinous display.

The stench of decay was suffocating, wrapping around them like a thick fog.

"Dear God," one officer murmured. His voice broke the silence yet was soon engulfed by the oppressive atmosphere.

Richardson pushed forward, his resolve solidified by the gruesomeness around him. In the far corner, a table held an assortment of tools, each one stained and worn. Mixed among them, disturbingly arranged, were relics of Falls's victims—personal items enshrined like trophies of his twisted conquests. This was no longer just a raid; it had become an exorcism of the demons that plagued their city.

"Evidence bag over here," Richardson called out, his voice steady despite the bile rising in his throat. Every photograph taken, every piece of evidence preserved, would ensure Falls's prosecution was ironclad. This monster would no longer sow terror unchecked.

Jason Falls was found upstairs, cowering behind a cluttered desk. His eyes were wild with the realization that the walls of his perverted sanctuary were closing in. Handcuffs clicked into place, his arrest marking a significant, desperately needed victory for the force.

As Falls was led away, Richardson surveyed the chaotic scene around them, taking in the silent gratitude of his team and the solemn nods that signified a job well done. There it was. The answer as to why Stacy Rhymes was always one step ahead. On the walls were pictures of her and Jason as children and adults. Stacy was Jason's older sister.

The city had been drowning in darkness, and tonight they had struck a critical blow against the malevolence that sought to consume it. He stepped out into the night, the oppressive gloom giving way to a rare sliver of hope.

THIRTEEN

SENTENCING

The judge's cough echoed through the solemn courtroom, a series of wet, choked sounds that permeated the tense atmosphere. It was enough to trigger a brief recess, allowing the judge to step out and catch his breath, leaving behind a wash of murmured conversations and rustling papers. Eric seized the opportunity to try and catch Mason's attention.

Eric leaned forward, his eyes flickering with an almost desperate gleam as he approached the defendant's bench. "Mason remember the promise I made you? To make you a famous artist?" Despite his low pitch, his voice carried an intensity that cut through the courtroom chatter.

Mason, his face a canvas of distress, glared at Eric. Strands of his hair clung to his damp forehead, and his eyes reflected a mix of disbelief and agony. "Eric, now? Of all times? My life is hanging by a thread here; can't you see that?" His voice quivered with a blend of anger and fear, his body rigid with tension.

For a moment, the courtroom seemed to hold its breath. Eric's face transformed, his eyes sharpening with resolve. "I've been killing, Mason," he confessed, almost triumphantly. "To increase the value of your paintings. Each body I leave behind magnifies your worth."

Mason's world shifted on its axis. His mind raced, pulling at threads of memories with Eric—moments of shared dreams and whispered ambitions now soiled by the revelation. Their bond, once a wellspring of inspiration, was now poisoned. His throat tightened, and a surge of panic threatened to crush him. A fierce mixture of guilt and horror flooded over him in waves, almost drowning his ability to breathe.

How many times had he marveled at their apparent synchronicity, mistaking Eric's praises for genuine admiration of his art, not realizing the monstrous price paid for every compliment? His career was built on a foundation of deceit and bloodshed. Now it felt like a noose tightening around his neck.

Mason's memories of his youthful ambitions flickered like scenes from an old film. From sketching under blankets with a flashlight to those late-night conversations where Eric had fueled his dream of greatness, he had always felt destined for more. Now, the very man who had nurtured those dreams stood exposed as their destroyer.

With trembling hands, Mason gripped the edge of the bench. He had always marveled at how Eric could be both his fiercest critic and greatest supporter, never suspecting the sinister undercurrents that shaped his zealous encouragement. The realization that his fame—his so-called success—was stained with innocent blood filled him with an overwhelming despair.

The bailiff's voice shattered the haunting silence, calling the courtroom back to order. It was a jarring contrast to the storm brewing in Mason's mind. The courtroom gradually fell silent as the session was to resume, but inside Mason, the tempest raged on, ruthless and unrelenting.

THE ATMOSPHERE IN THE COURTROOM SHIFTED ONCE THE judge returned to his chair. Once seated, he apologized for the delay. Murmurs of suppressed tension rippled through the room like an invisible tide. The crackle of anxiety intertwined with the delicate, muffled coughs that punctuated the air. Faces, a mosaic of discomfort and anticipation, leaned forward, waiting for the judge's gavel to signal the resumption of order. Most of them were family members of the victims, cloaked in the heavy mantle of their grief, eyes hollow from sleepless nights and swollen from endless tears.

Mason Mind stood abruptly, his heart a storm of conflicting

emotions. His voice sliced through the air, reverberating off the somber wood panels of the courtroom. "Your Honor, I have something to say about the killings!" he shouted, desperation soaking every word, seeking to catch the attention of the gavel that had defined his fate thus far.

For a breathless moment, the room fell silent, the tension a tangible thread binding everyone in place. Then, from the rows of spectators, a figure rose. The father of one of the victims, his face a mask of desolation and anger, glistening trails of tears zigzagging down his cheeks, moved with a determination that seemed to drive him beyond the limits of his grief. His trembling hand revealed a chrome-plated .40-caliber pistol. The courtroom lights glinted off the weapon as if mocking the solemnity of this institution.

Like wind gathering before a storm, gasps of horror arose from all corners of the courtroom. The gunman's sobs mingled with his ragged breaths as he aimed at Mason, screaming something incoherent yet heartbreaking. Just as the judge's gavel struck the sound block, the metallic bite of the gunshot clawed through the air, and Mason felt the savage impact in his chest. Blood blossomed on his shirt, a ghastly flower of pain, as he collapsed to the floor.

Chaos erupted instantly. People scrambled, tripping over each other, seats clattering as if possessed by the collective dread of the courtroom's inhabitants. Mothers shielded their children; others dove for cover under rows of benches. An eerie wail of despair from the shooter was punctuated by his cries. The courtroom had become a theater of panic.

The judge, momentarily paralyzed by fear, ducked beneath his chair, the reverberations of the gunshot still ringing in his ears. Peeking out cautiously, he saw the bailiffs, their discipline overcoming their initial shock, converge on the shooter. They subdued him with swift precision, wrenching the gun from his grip and dragging him away, his cries now a muted echo in the cacophony of pandemonium.

Mason laid on the floor, blood pooling around him as his breath came in shallow gasps. His life's accomplishments, flashes of fleeting moments of pride and artistic triumph, rushed through his mind, interspersed with nostalgic images of childhood: the smell of his mother's baking, the sound of laughter with his best friend Isaac Reynolds, the sight of his first completed painting. The irony of these memories, so vivid in his final moments, weighed heavily on him.

In the midst of this turmoil, the societal impact of the murders unfolded like a grim tapestry. The courtroom, once a symbol of order and justice, had become a stage for tragedy, illustrating the fragile veneer of civilization. The fragile trust in the judicial system, which had been strained by the relentless killings, was now shattered as easily as glass. The community's collective trauma resonated within these walls, with each crack of gunfire echoing the breaking of their spirits. The scent of gunpowder filled the air, mingling with the metallic tang of blood, a sensory testament to the evening's horror.

Mason's vision blurred as he continued gasping, the sounds of the courtroom fading into a distant roar. He could see Eric's face in his mind, clear and accusing, as voices beyond the immediate chaos called out, "Eric, Eric, Eric." The refrain became a haunting chorus, enveloping Mason in a final numbness, pulling him deeper into the void.

His eyes darkened, the world becoming a canvas of shadows, the last remnants of light receding as the screams melded into the growing silence.

ERIC'S EYES FLUTTERED OPEN AND CLOSED LIKE A FAILING engine struggling to turn over. Each blink brought him fleeting glimpses of a courtroom now tinged with chaos. He tried to rise but felt an anchor of dizziness dragging him down. Clutching his chest, he could feel the sticky warmth of his blood-soaked shirt pressing against his skin, an unsettling reminder of the violence that had just exploded around him.

The room swayed like a ship caught in a storm as panic crept into his chest, swelling and bursting into severe muscle spasms. The convulsions forced his body to arc violently, driving his head onto the unforgiving edge of the court bench. Pain erupted, a piercing starburst in his skull, and he felt the skin tear apart, a line of searing agony. Blood streamed down his face, mingling with the earlier stain on his shirt, obscuring his vision with streaks of crimson.

Through the throbbing pain, Eric struggled to understand where he was or what had happened. His mind felt like a shattered mirror—fragmented reflections of Mason's trials and the courtroom's pandemonium whirling in its depths but never forming a complete picture. The smell of antiseptics and the echoing footsteps of horrified spectators were more acute than ever, making his disorientation even more visceral.

He felt like he was floating on the brink of consciousness, thoughts flickering like a faulty projector. Each flash carried snippets of courtroom chaos, Mason's ashen face, the judge's gavel falling like a final fate, and the madman's tear-stricken eyes holding a deadly resolve. The tension between his own terror and the crushing responsibility for his nephew's fate was starting to suffocate him. His breath hitched as he tried to piece together if he had blacked out yet again. The cycles felt never-ending, a carousel of horror he couldn't escape.

"Did I blackout again?" His voice was a rasp, barely audible over the murmurs and footfalls around him.

Simone's presence anchored him, even as his world threatened to drift away. Her calmness felt like a lifeline in this emotional tempest. She knelt at his side, the hem of her pristine suit brushing the courtroom floor now stained with chaos.

"Yes, Eric. You passed out after being sentenced," she explained, her voice a soft, steady current cutting through his storm. Her hand rested gently on his shoulder, pulling him slightly from the abyss of his panic.

His spirit dwindled further, battling the anguish that pressed him down. Each memory of Mason seemed like a brick in the wall of guilt and fear that had encased him. The courtroom buzzed with the sounds of panic and chaos, underscoring the melodrama playing out in his own life.

Eric couldn't shake off the creeping sense of failure. He had failed Mason. Each passing second seemed to pronounce his inability to prevent these horrifying events, their family bonds fraying into ragged edges, disintegrating under the weight of accusations and bloodshed.

The pain in his chest synced with every beat of his heart, infusing his physical agony with his emotional despair. He could not tell which pain was worse—the unbearable spasms that gripped his ribs or the constant surge of images and memories of Mason, whose life now hung precariously by the thread of the court's decisions.

Simone's presence offered a thin veneer of stability in his unraveling world. Her calm demeanor and steady words contrasted sharply with the turmoil tearing at his soul. Her explanations were mere whispers against the roaring storm inside him, yet they were necessary, grounding him amid his otherwise fragmentary reality.

To breathe became a battle, each gasp a struggle against the insidious despair gnawing at him. His fractured thoughts kept returning to Mason —the intense courtroom scenes merging with fragments of happier days, his nephew's smiling face, the beginnings of his art career, all tainted now by the sour decay of their present nightmare. It was a struggle to even muster memories of what mattered before this maelstrom hit them.

He glanced up, seeing Simone's lips move, though her words now blurred into the white noise of his panic. Tears pooled in his eyes, distorting the view of her concerned face. With an almost herculean effort, he forced himself to listen and anchor himself to her steadiness.

"You're not alone, Eric. But you need to stay with me here," she said, her voice cutting through the noise in his mind.

For a moment, he clung to her words, using them to fend off the panic threatening to consume him whole. She was his rock, and yet, he knew, even the strongest rocks erode under relentless waves, much like the court-room walls that now felt cold and cavernous around him.

In the distance, the echoing hallways swallowed the last remnants of courtroom chaos. Mason's name lingered on his lips like an incantation, mingling with silent screams as his vision blurred. Eric's crisis of sanity loomed large, trapping him in a cycle he feared he might never break free from. In this fraught moment, he could only futilely grasp at the elusive fragments of comprehension, half-drowned in his own abyssal despair. Tomorrow seemed farther away than ever before.

SIMONE SAT RIGIDLY IN THE STERILE ROOM, FLUORESCENT lights casting an unforgiving glare on every corner. Eric's face had the hollow look of someone who had lived through too many nightmares, his eyes flitting nervously as if seeking an escape. Simone took a deep breath, steeling herself against the whirlwind of emotions bubbling just under her composed facade.

"You kept repeating Mason's name while you were unconscious, Eric," Simone began, her voice wavering. "They've confirmed your sentencing to a mental asylum."

Eric's brow furrowed, his expression a tapestry of confusion and distress. "Mason... again?" he muttered, more to himself than to Simone.

"I become Mason when I paint, Simone. It's like I lose myself entirely, but when I'm not painting, it's like Mason doesn't even exist. How long am I supposed to be there?"

Simone swallowed hard, the weight of the situation pressing down on her. She had seen fractures in people's psyches before, but Eric's was a chasm that seemed to grow deeper with every word he spoke. "Until the doctors believe you're fit to leave, Eric. That might be a long time. As long as it takes."

Eric's eyes shone with unshed tears, his voice trembling. "I never wanted this to happen. I thought... I thought if I could just help him, his work would finally get the recognition it deserved. People needed to see how brilliant Mason was. But it got out of hand. It became a part of me— a dark part I couldn't control. But the girl messed everything up; she said my paintings were terrible. Through my eyes, they were beautiful. So, I removed her eyes because I wanted to see my art through her eyes."

Simone fought back the shivers crawling up her spine, her own hands starting to tremble as Eric revealed the unsettling rationale behind his actions. Each word pierced through the fragile comfort she tried to maintain. "Do you understand what you're saying, Eric? How dangerous this is?"

Eric's gaze locked onto hers, filled with a mix of fear and a twisted sense of pride. "I saw it, Simone. I saw my future while I was passed out. Mason's future. I have to finish what we started, even if it means staying here. I know what's coming. I've always known."

The room seemed to grow colder, the clinical beeps and hums of the facility fading into the background as Simone processed Eric's chilling assertion. She saw something new in this eight-year old boy—a determined glint that spoke of unfinished business. Eric's last words hung in the air like a dark omen, their unsettling implications crawling into Simone's mind, consuming her with dread and an acute sense of urgency.

Simone's heart pounded against her ribs, a silent scream of terror at the possible future she glimpsed through Eric's tortured eyes. Would the asylum be enough to keep his demons at bay, or would they fester, waiting for the moment they could be unleashed upon the world? If Eric could so easily shift between identities, how could anyone be sure he wouldn't evolve into something more monstrous?

Eric leaned back, a cruel smile playing on his lips. He seemed almost victorious, a boy who had come to terms with his fractured reality. "You're afraid, Simone, aren't you?" he whispered, voice low and dangerous. "A part of me rejoices in that fear. Mason's fear. My fear. It's all the same, feeding off each other, growing stronger."

Simone couldn't deny it. She was terrified. Not just for what Eric had done, but for what he was yet to do. "It's not too late, Eric. You can still get help. You don't have to let Mason control you."

But Eric's eyes were already lost in some distant vision, his mouth set in a determined line. The quiet resolution in his tone as he spoke again chilled Simone to the bone. "I've already seen my future, Simone. Mason and I—we have a destiny to fulfill. And nothing, not even this asylum, can hold us back."

The words hung heavily in the air, unspoken shadows gathering in the sterile room.

ACKNOWLEDGMENTS

A special thanks goes to my extraordinary wife, Charmain, whose unwavering support and belief in me motivated me to bring to life the thought I had in my head. I had shelved this idea, but she reminded me that a great movie is just a thought until that vision is followed. Her love and encouragement were the driving force behind this book.

I want to express my heartfelt gratitude to my children De', Bre, Alyssa, Jesi, ShaVon, Shacondra, Ayshia, and Lai'. Their love and support have been a constant source of motivation, inspiring me to strive to be a better person, a better father, and a mentor. Their presence in my life has been a blessing and a driving force behind this book.

I want to thank my sister, Dr. Latrice Mitchell of Unwritten, for helping me adequately express my thoughts in my writing. She was a force in verbiage, critiquing, editing, and constructive criticism. I also want to thank my editor, Dr. Sabin P. Duncan of Fielding Books, for the continual support and education needed to complete my goal successfully. I will always be grateful for these two.

I want to thank my parents, Linda and Vondell Sr., for the unconditional love and support a child needs to go out into the world with his ideas and goals and for wanting to become someone in the community. Also, I thank my extended mother, Eulalia, for the educational foundation that allowed me to want to be better scholastically.

As I present this book, my first project, I am filled with anticipation for the future. I hope that everyone enjoys reading it as much as I have enjoyed writing it, and I look forward to sharing many more projects with you.

www.ingramcontent.com/pod-product-compliance
Lightning Source LLC
Chambersburg PA
CBHW050502110726
47899CB00003B/1046